Child
of the
Sea

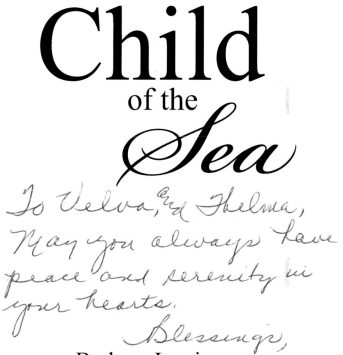

To Velva, and Thelma,
May you always have
peace and serenity in
your hearts.
            Blessings,

Barbara Larriva

            Barbara Larriva

Child of the Sea

Book and Cover Design: Veronica A. Martinez
Cover Image © Francesca Bianco

For information regarding permission, write to Tau publishing, Attention: Permissions Dept, 1422 East Edgemont Avenue, Phoenix, AZ 85006

ISBN-10:1-935257-08-0
ISBN-13: 978-1-935257-08-0

First Edition: March 2009
10 9 8 7 6 5 4 3 2 1

For re-orders and other inspirational books and materials visit our website at Tau-publishing.com

Published and Printed in the USA by:

Tau-publishing.com
Words and Works of Inspiration

To Mothers Everywhere...

Child of the Sea:

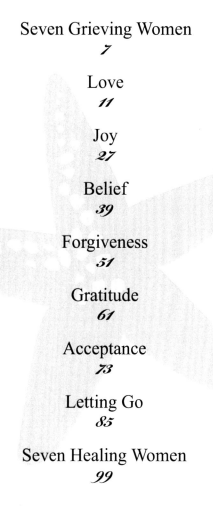

1

Seven Grieving Women

onths after the killer wave struck their fishing village, leaving black holes where hearts had once been, seven grieving women stood on the white sandy beach looking out into the deep. Madhur, the elder, scanned the bereaved faces of her friends and shook her head sadly. Together they had cried enough tears to fill an additional ocean. She didn't know whether it had been a curse or a blessing that their lives had been spared. All seven had been working at the tourist hotel high up on the hill that fateful day when the ocean claimed their children.

As the breeze lifted their long colorful skirts, the thin material wrapped itself around their strong, sun-browned legs. Wisps of hair came loose and the women brushed the strands out of their sunken eyes. Kirti nudged her friend Kamalika standing next to her, and pointed vigorously at the now calm water. The women used their hands to shield their eyes from the bright afternoon sun glancing off the rippling waves.

Amazed, they realized that floating toward them was a young girl clinging to a splintered piece of driftwood. As one, the seven women held up their skirts and waded into the surf. Eager hands captured the debris and pulled the child to safety.

She was dark-skinned. Black, curly hair tangled with seaweed hung down her back. Encircling her neck was a silver chain with a tiny puffed heart dangling in the center. She appeared to be about seven years old.

Madhur reached out and smoothed back a stray ringlet and studied the young face. The child's eyes mirrored the color of the ocean. And the depths of those aquamarine eyes revealed a wisdom far beyond her years.

"What's your name, child? Where are you from?" Madhur asked.

The girl's eyes turned cloudy as she stared from one to the other and then slowly shook her head. A few seconds later, she pulled her tattered dress around herself, curled up on the warm sand and fell asleep. Hema removed her green-fringed shawl and covered the child.

The seven women, acquainted with everyone in the village, knew she was not one of them.

After studying the sleeping child for some time, the seven women looked at each other. They made a pact not to tell anyone how they found the girl. They would raise her themselves. Amidst all the grief and sorrow in the village, they were sure that no one would pay heed. As if she knew what was being decided, the girl smiled sweetly in her sleep.

The women huddled together, their dark heads touching. They separated and gestured to each other, speaking sometimes in whispers, sometimes loudly. When they came to a decision, it was Kirti, the one who first spotted the girl, who spoke.

She looked from the sleeping child to the deep ocean, then back to her friends. "Yes, it is fitting we name her for the sea. She shall be known as Oceana."

Agreeing, the women nodded and moved away from the child. They squatted in a circle and put their heads together once more.

"Which of us will she live with?" asked Ushma, a slight woman, fidgeting with nervousness.

"Me. I'm the oldest," responded Madhur, rubbing her tough, weather-lined face.

But the others shook their heads.

"I'm the youngest," said Jasmira. "I suppose I should be the one to care for her." But her mouth drooped at the corners contradicting her words.

Again, the others shook their heads.

"I lost the most children," a sad-eyed Hema whispered, swiping at the tears that ran down her face. She put her head in her hands and wept.

The other six heads continued to shake.

The women resumed their discussion of the child. They huddled for several more minutes until finally they agreed that Oceana would live among all seven, spending one month with each of them.

"And what will she call us?" asked Gulika.

After a lengthy discussion, Madhur held up her hand and made a suggestion. "Let us gather seven twigs of different lengths. The one who chooses the longest stick will be called Mama One and we will work up from there until we end with Mama Seven. We will all be her mother." The other women eagerly nodded in agreement and set off to search for twigs.

And so it came about that Oceana would have seven Mamas. And each of the seven women would relinquish a part of her grief to make a space in her heart for this girl who came to them from the same mysterious place their children were taken—the sea.

Love

Mama One

Kamalika lifted the basket of laundry she had picked up earlier from the tourist hotel and balanced it on the thick black hair coiled around her head. With a straight back she trudged down to the stream. Setting the basket on the ground, she scrubbed a blouse and laid it out to dry. She then plucked a soiled shirt from the basket.

As she washed the shirt, her wandering thoughts settled on Oceana, who would be with her for four whole weeks. Although she would never admit this to the others, Kamalika had secretly hoped to choose the shortest twig and be Mama Seven. She wasn't ready to have another child in her house, even for just a month. Children needed love. She had none to give. Her heart had shriveled up when the killer wave struck.

Although her heart had opened a crack when Oceana first came to them out of the sea, Kamalika was unable to keep it open. Like a clam it snapped shut again. Her losses to the killer wave were not greater than those of the others. But without her two sons and her husband, her life was empty. She had built a wall around herself to keep everyone out.

"Can I help?" Oceana asked, breaking into Kamalika's thoughts. The girl tucked her tattered dress between her knees as she squatted next to the woman.

Kamalika looked at the child, who had been with her for three days, and snickered. "And how do you think you could help?"

Oceana raised her eyes and scrunched up her nose, deep in thought. "I could spread the clothes out to dry after you wash them."

"With those dirty hands? I'd just have to re-wash everything," Kamalika said, dismissing Oceana with a wave.

The child persisted. "I'll wash them," she said and leaned over the stream to splash water on her hands. As she did so, she also wet the clothes that were almost dry.

"Now look what you've done," Kamalika complained, moving Oceana away with a free hand.

Oceana plopped down on the ground. "Well, maybe I could sing."

Kamalika gasped. Tears pricked her eyelids.

"I'm sorry I made you sad, Mama One," Oceana said, touching the woman's shoulder with her small hand.

Kamalika looked at Oceana and the tears resurfaced. "Go. Just leave me alone."

The girl got to her feet and ran off.

Memories flooded Kamalika. She pounded her fists on the ground to ease the pain in her heart. Her youngest son had always sung to her, making up songs so she would laugh. But there was no laughter now, because there was no love. Her empty, closed, shrunken heart no longer had room for love.

She had been in the safety of the tourist hotel with the six other women when the killer wave slammed into their lives. While she had been ironing sheets, her husband and boys had been out in a small fishing boat. Their broken bodies had been washed away and she never had the chance to hold them or say good-bye.

Kamalika wiped her eyes with the hem of her dress and then furiously slapped more of the tourists' fancy clothes against the rocks. After spreading the clean clothes out on branches to dry, she sat on her haunches. She looked around for Oceana and felt a pang of guilt. Why had she been so abrupt with the child? She wondered where the girl had come from and if somewhere a mother was missing Oceana just as much as she missed her sons. Or had the sea also swallowed up Oceana's family?

An hour later Kamalika touched the garments, making sure they were dry before folding them. She once again balanced the wash basket on her head and walked back to her makeshift dwelling. Setting the basket down when she entered the room, she spotted Oceana sitting on her sleeping mat, sliding the heart back and forth along the silver chain around her neck. To Kamalika's relief, Oceana turned and smiled sweetly.

A whimper from the side of the dusty path suddenly caught Oceana's attention. She hurried out to investigate the sound and found a small dog lying on his side, struggling to get up. Oceana squatted down next to him and shrugged out of her dress. She scrunched up the threadbare material and put it under the dog's head.

From the doorway, Kamalika watched Oceana, now clad in her underwear. "Leave the dog be. And pick up your dress. It's getting dirty."

Oceana's head was bowed as she ran her hand over the dog's matted fur. He shivered, despite the warmth of the early afternoon sun. "He's sick, Mama One. We have to help him." She looked over at the woman who stood watching with her arms crossed.

Kamalika shook her head. "Leave him. Let somebody else take care of him."

"Who, Mama One?"

The woman threw her arms up in the air. "I don't know, but not you or me," she said as she turned and began preparing lunch.

After several minutes Oceana leaned down, kissed the whimpering dog on his head, and walked to the dwelling.

"You forgot your dress," Kamalika said.

"The dog needs it."

Kamalika shook her head impatiently. A sick dog meant nothing to her. "Hurry and eat. I have to take the laundry to the hotel."

"Why don't you want to help him?" Oceana asked softly.

Her tolerance gone, Kamalika shouted, "Because nobody helps me. I have no one and I'm all alone."

Oceana gently touched Kamalika's shoulder. "I'll take care of you."

Moved by the child's simple words, but unwilling to show it, Kamalika poured some soup into a chipped bowl. "Go," she told the girl tersely. "Take it to the dog."

Kamalika watched from the doorway as Oceana hurried out with a slab of bread and the bowl of soup in her hands. Kneeling by the dog, she lay his head on her lap. After dipping a small piece of bread in the soup, she put the moistened food in his mouth. The hungry dog swallowed the bread and looked up at Oceana with soulful brown eyes.

Kamalika shook her head and left with the basket of

laundry. Now she'd have to get a dress for Oceana from one of the other women.

Later that week, Kamalika tired and aching from bending over an iron all day walked into her house. "What's this?" she demanded.

Oceana had brought the dog inside and the pup was sleeping on her mat. "Get that dog out of here," Kamalika demanded, pointing to the animal. "I told you someone else would take care of him."

Oceana's dark hair hung in ringlets around her face. "But nobody came, Mama One," Oceana said, her eyes glistening with tears.

Rigid, Kamalika said, "Now!"

The girl carried the dog outside and sat with him on her lap in the shade. When he fell asleep, she lifted him gently and placed him on the ground. Then, with her bare hands she dug a hole for the dog to sleep in. He would stay cool in the dirt. Oceana wiped her hands on the dress Mama One had found for her and hiked up the sleeves that kept slipping off her shoulders.

The next morning, Kamalika awoke and looked over toward Oceana's sleeping mat. It was empty. She padded to the door and looked outside. Oceana and the dog were curled up together, sleeping. Silly child, thought Kamalika. When the dog recovers he'll probably bite Oceana. Then she'll see.

Snickering, Kamalika turned and went inside to prepare morning tea. But her thoughts were scrambled. She felt guilty, impatient and confused.

When breakfast was ready, Kamalika called Oceana inside. Obediently, the child moved the dog away from the warmth of her body and bent over to whisper something in his ear. The dog's tongue lashed out and licked Oceana's face. Laughing, she jumped to her feet and skipped over to Kamalika.

After their rice and tea, Oceana stood up and said, "Let's go outside and sit in the sun."

"I'm too busy to sit around doing nothing."

"Please," Oceana coaxed, tugging on Kamalika's arm.

Kamalika sighed heavily but gave in to the girl. One brick at a time, Oceana was slowly chipping away at the wall the woman had built. They sat side by side on the ground in companionable silence. Then Kamalika spoke. "You must forget about the dog. Let him go."

Oceana's blue-green eyes widened and she shook her head. "Where would he go? Who would take care of him?"

Kamalika ignored Oceana's questions. "The truth is, I don't understand your love for this animal."

Oceana stared intently at Kamalika. "It's a feeling that comes from my heart," she replied, tapping her chest. "Why don't you feel it, too?" she asked, touching Kamalika's breastbone.

The woman sat back on her haunches, drawn into Oceana's gaze. "I don't know," she whispered.

Kamalika had another load of clean laundry ready to take to the hotel.

"Can I go with you?" Oceana asked.

"No, you stay here," Kamalika told her. She saw the disappointed look on Oceana's face and sighed. "Oh, all right. Come along. But don't get under my feet. I don't want to have to wash all these clothes again."

Oceana nodded and walked silently beside Kamalika. The girl began to sing and then abruptly stopped after getting a disapproving look from the woman.

"Wait out here. I don't want any nosy questions from the other workers," Kamalika said as they neared the tourist hotel.

A half hour later, Kamalika came out of the hotel with a bag of clothes.

Oceana stood up and brushed the dust off the bottom of her dress. As they walked side by side, she asked, "Is that more wash?"

"No, the tourists gave me some of their clothes. I can cut them up and make a dress or two for you."

Oceana clapped her hands. "You'll make a dress for me?"

"Of course. Why are you so surprised?"

"Because you don't like me."

Kamalika abruptly stopped walking. "Whatever gave you that idea?" But in her heart she knew that what the girl had just said was true.

"You never touch me, or hug me." Oceana looked down at her bare feet. "And I always make you sad."

Kamalika reached out to lay a hand on Oceana's curly head, then pulled it back. "Nonsense," she muttered and resumed walking down the hill.

Later, Kamalika beckoned Oceana to come inside. "While it's still light enough, I want to cut the material to make the dresses. Stand up on that box so I can measure you," she instructed Oceana.

"Oh, what pretty material," Oceana exclaimed as she looked at the heap of dresses from the tourists and climbed up on the box. "I want that one," she said, pointing to a poppy-red dress with a border of small blue and white flowers embroidered around the hem.

"Pick another. I'm keeping that dress for myself."

"But I really like that one," Oceana said sullenly.

Unbending, Kamalika stood with her hands on her hips, her lips in a straight line.

Oceana then pointed to a blue dress.

"I'll cut the dress down and make you one just like it."

As the days moved on, Kamalika made Oceana five dresses. In time, as she fitted the child, she found herself taking Oceana's arm to turn her this way and that. Touching her wasn't as painful as it had been in the beginning. When Kamalika looked into Oceana's blue-green eyes, she realized another brick had been chipped away. She wondered about that.

When she gave Oceana the dresses, the child's eyes widened and she exclaimed, "You made the poppy-red dress for me!"

Kamalika smiled at Oceana's exuberance.

"But you wanted it for yourself," Oceana said.

Kamalika shrugged.

Oceana clapped her hands. "Thank you. Thank you. Thank you."

"Stop thanking me and acting as if I've given you a bag of sweets," Kamalika said irritably, resisting the temptation to gather the child in her arms.

"It's good manners to say thank you when someone gives you something," Oceana solemnly pointed out.

"So now you're going to teach me," Kamalika said, slamming her scissors down, making the table jiggle.

"Don't be silly, Mama One," Oceana answered, shaking her head. "Children don't teach grown-ups."

Kamalika looked at the child who stared up at her with beautiful eyes the deep color of the sea. Before Oceana came to them, Kamalika would have agreed. Today she wasn't so sure. For although Oceana acted like a little girl, many times her words were far advanced for a young child.

Several days later, Oceana was sitting outside the dwelling with the dog when Kamalika returned from work. "See," the girl said, "he's getting better. He can sit up now."

"I'm tired, Oceana. I don't want to hear about him." She plopped down next to Oceana. A few minutes later when Oceana started to again talk about the dog, Kamalika said,

"Don't you understand? That mongrel can't do anything for you."

"I don't want him to," Oceana replied simply. "I just want to help him."

Kamalika wouldn't let up. "And when he's better, he'll probably run away. He's not worth your trouble, Oceana. He's nothing."

Oceana shook her head. "He's living and he's breathing so he must be something."

Kamalika's eyes rolled upward.

"He has a heart that thumps just like yours and mine," insisted the girl. "I can feel it when I pet him."

"So what does that mean?" Kamalika's head began to throb.

"It means I have to love him." She turned to face Kamalika. "If somebody loved you and took care of you, would you love the dog?"

"I'll never love anything again. Everything I love gets taken away."

"But, if…"

Kamalika raised her hands to silence Oceana. "There are no *ifs*."

In the middle of the night some days later, Oceana crawled over to where Kamalika was sleeping. She put her small head close to the older woman's. "Mama One, I'm afraid. I had a bad dream. Can I sleep with you?"

Kamalika sat up and pointed to Oceana's corner. "Go back to sleep. There's nothing to be afraid of."

"Please," Oceana whispered, not moving.

A sigh escaped Kamalika's lips. "All right. But lie quietly." She scooted over on the sleeping mat to give Oceana room. Aware of the child lying next to her, Kamalika couldn't fall back to sleep. Oceana's arm flung out and touched

Kamalika. The woman pulled away. But slowly she let her hand find Oceana's and her fingers laced with the young girl's hand. With a smile on her face, Kamalika fell asleep.

The next morning she awoke to find Oceana cuddled next to her. Backing away from the sleeping child, she quickly got up. While she puttered around the small room, the guilty feelings that had plagued her returned.

As she looked down at Oceana, now curled up in a ball, Kamalika felt a tug in her heart. She quickly turned away, busying herself with tea-making. But she couldn't help peeking over her shoulder at the sleeping child.

While Oceana slept, Kamalika broke some crackers and put them in a bowl of soup. She took it to the dog, who lapped it up hungrily.

When Oceana awakened, Kamalika gave her hot tea and bread. The young girl sat at the rickety table made from scraps of wood and ate in silence, a puzzled look on her face. "Why was I sleeping on your mat?" she finally asked.

"You don't remember? You had a bad dream and didn't want to sleep alone."

Oceana's eyes lit up and she put her small hands to her mouth. "And you let me?"

"You were afraid."

"Thank you," Oceana said, and then abruptly covered her mouth with her hands. "Don't be mad at me. I wasn't trying to teach you."

Again, Kamalika wasn't so sure.

When Oceana went outside to see the dog, she noticed the empty bowl. Running back inside, she cried, "You fed the dog!"

Kamalika shrugged and looked away. "Just a few leftovers."

Oceana's eyes were aglow. "But you always tell me there's

not enough food…"

"Go outside and play. The dog's lonely." She gently touched Oceana's shoulder.

Oceana started to speak, but Kamalika silenced her. "Go," she said, scooting the girl out the door. When Kamalika turned around, a smile lifted the corners of her mouth.

One evening after the laundry had been washed and dried and delivered to the hotel, Kamalika suggested they go to the beach. A terrible sadness had come over her and she needed the comfort of the sea where her family rested. She and Oceana sat in silence for many minutes watching the waves lap at the shoreline, leaving behind frothy bubbles. The dog sat quietly at their feet.

As tears slid down Kamalika's sad face, she made no move to wipe them away. Her heartache was too great. She could think of nothing but her family, loved ones she would never see again.

"Did I make you sad again, Mama One?" Oceana asked, touching the woman's shoulder with her small hand.

To her own surprise, Kamalika pulled Oceana to her side. "No, little one. I'm thinking of my sons who are forever lost to me. Some days I don't think I can bear the pain. You, Oceana, bring me some comfort." She looked down at the girl. "But no one can take the place of my two little boys." She began to weep again.

Oceana turned to Kamalika and wiped her tears away. "Can I be your daughter?"

The woman shook her head. "My heart has no room for a daughter."

"I'm small. I won't take up much room," the girl said softly.

Kamalika smiled in spite of herself. "I wish I could open my heart to you, but I can't. My grief is too much for me to bear."

Oceana touched her chest. "My heart is big enough for you and your family."

Kamalika bowed her head until her forehead rested on Oceana's curly hair. When darkness overtook them, Kamalika put her arms around Oceana who was still sitting by her side. "Thank you," she whispered.

"For what?" The young girl turned to face the older woman.

"For showing me love," Kamalika said softly. She stood up and reached out to Oceana. "Come, let's go home." Hand in hand they walked through the moonless night, the dog prancing beside them.

To Kamalika's great surprise, she began to look forward to coming home from work and watching Oceana play with the dog. The girl always gave herself totally to the comfort and pleasure of the puppy. Kamalika began to realize that even though Oceana had said she didn't want anything from the animal, he was giving back the love he was receiving.

She decided to talk to Oceana about it. That evening after supper, they sat on the ground outside their dwelling. The dog romped and played with a stick Oceana tossed just far enough for him to dash out, retrieve it, and drop it at her feet.

"Tell me about your connection to this dog, Oceana," Kamalika said.

The girl frowned. "I don't know what you mean."

Kamalika leaned back against some splintered pieces of wood stacked alongside the dwelling. "Why did you help him when you first saw him? Did you feel sorry for him?"

Oceana thought for a while. "He needed a family."

"A family?" Oceana tossed another stick for the dog to chase. "To get better he needed to belong to someone. Someone who loved him." At that moment, the last rays of sunshine broke through the clustering clouds and fell on Oceana's upturned face. It was aglow with light.

Kamalika sucked in her breath, blinked, and in that moment the clouds recaptured the sun, snatching away the light. Recovering, she said, "And who do you belong to, Oceana?"

The girl smiled and threw her arms out wide. "To everything and everybody."

"And what does that mean?" Oceana's comments never failed to amaze Kamalika.

Oceana giggled and covered her mouth with her hands. She shrugged. "I don't know. It just came to me."

"And if the dog went away, would you be unhappy?"

"I don't think so."

"Why not?" Kamalika leaned closer to Oceana.

"Because he wouldn't need me anymore. And I'd find another dog, or a fish, or a bird to love."

Kamalika tucked those words away to digest at a later time.

It was almost the end of the month with Oceana when Kamalika realized she had made a complete turnabout in her thinking. She didn't want to let the girl or the dog go. But of course, she knew she had to. An agreement with the other women had been made.

During the last week, Kamalika spent all her free time with Oceana. "Thank you again for the dresses," Oceana said and quickly covered her mouth as she and Kamalika walked the beach.

Instead of reprimanding Oceana, Kamalika smiled and gently touched the girl's head. "It was my pleasure to make them for you and to see you happy." She sat down on the warm sand.

"But I was happy before the dresses."

Kamalika studied the young girl. "Why are you happy,

Oceana?"

"Because I'm here."

"Here on the beach?" Kamalika asked.

Oceana shook her head, her curls flying in her face. "No, just here."

"But what makes you happy?"

Oceana twirled in the sand, her bare feet kicking up grains, her arms outstretched. "Everything." The dog ran in circles around her.

"You weren't happy when I yelled at you or ignored you," Kamalika said.

"Yes I was. In here." She touched her heart. "I love your two sons," Oceana said suddenly.

Kamalika's breath caught in her throat. "You didn't know them. Why do you say you love them?"

Oceana shrugged. "I don't know. The words just came to me."

"Don't say things you don't mean. That's hurtful."

"But I do mean it, Mama One."

"I don't understand you, Oceana. You're a mystery to me."

Oceana sat down next to Kamalika. "I love you too, Mama One."

Kamalika began to cry.

"I'm sorry I made you sad again," the girl apologized, dismayed.

"No, Oceana. These are happy tears." She gathered the child in her arms and rocked her back and forth.

After a few moments of silence, Kamalika asked, "Will you take the dog when you go to Mama Two?"

"Would you like to keep him?"

Kamalika nodded. "I'll take good care of him." Remembering the child's earlier words, she added, "I'll be his family."

"I think he would like to stay with you," Oceana said, smiling. Turning to the dog, she asked, "Do you want to stay with Mama One?"

The dog wagged his tail in reply, and Kamalika smiled.

As the evening began to chill, Kamalika held Oceana closer. When the moon slid out from behind a cloud, she lifted the girl's curly hair and whispered in her ear, "I love you, Oceana."

With those words, the wall around Kamalika crumbled.

The little girl reached up and touched Kamalika's face. "Is your heart open?"

"Yes, my daughter."

Oceana sighed happily and leaned against Kamalika. Entwining her fingers with the older woman's, Oceana looked up, her face radiant in the moonlight.

Then from a place deep in her heart filled with love, Kamalika said, "Sing to me, Oceana. Sing to me."

And Oceana sang.

Joy

Mama Two

Hema sat in the dark, staring at the blank wall before her. Tears ran down her haggard face, and her straggly hair hung in clumps. The sea had taken all five of her children and her husband. The killer wave had blackened her beating heart forever. Hema wanted only one thing now—to die.

She wondered why she had promised to take Oceana for a month. If she couldn't bear to look at the orphan children hanging around the tourist hotel, how would she handle living with a child who would constantly remind her of her dead children? But Hema had made a commitment, and she would honor it.

So when she heard Oceana singing as she came up the path, Hema tried to pull herself together even though a feeling of despair overwhelmed her. She forced a smile on her face, but couldn't stop the tears from falling.

"Mama Two, what's the matter?" Oceana said, running to the woman. "Are you sad because I'm going to stay with you?" Oceana looked up into the woman's sorrowful eyes.

Hema shook her head. "I just can't stop thinking of my children. I wonder if they called out for me when they were pulled into the sea." Her mouth quivered and she began to sob, then quickly swiped at her tears with her bare arm.

"Tell me about your children," Oceana said as she helped wipe away Hema's tears with her small hand. "Maybe it will make you feel better."

At first Hema protested. Then she took a deep breath and nodded. Maybe the child was right—maybe talking would help.

And so Hema sat back in a wobbly chair with Oceana kneeling beside her. For the first time since the tragedy, she spoke of her four sons and her only daughter. "While I was at the hotel working, my children were helping their father weave fishing nets because his fingers were twisted from arthritis. They loved their father and they loved the sea, especially my daughter." Hema stifled a sob. Oceana took the distraught woman's hand and held it tightly. Composing herself, Hema continued her tale.

When she finished, Oceana asked quietly, "Do you think there might be a tiny place in your heart for me?"

Hema shook her head sadly. "The killer wave swept my heart clean and left a black hole. I have no heart anymore."

Oceana put her small hand on Hema's chest. "Yes you do. I can feel it beating."

Hema smiled weakly at Oceana. "I wish I knew how to make it stop so I could be with my family."

Oceana's eyes misted. "I wish you could be happy again,

Mama Two."

"Why? What is there to be happy about?"

"The other Mamas love you. You have a house. And food."

Hema swung her arms wide, her gaze taking in the makeshift house with its lopsided roof. "I'd give it all up if I could have my children and husband back."

"But you can't, Mama Two. Yesterday's gone. There's only now."

Hema looked away from Oceana with downcast eyes and spoke in a near whisper, "You don't know my heartache, Oceana. How could you? You're just a child." She shook her head sadly. "My heart, my soul is black. Everything is black. I am shrouded in blackness."

Oceana looked pensive and then said, "Maybe we could poke a hole in the black. Make a teeny space and fill it with happy. I'll help you." Excitement shone from her eyes as she looked up at Hema.

"Thank you for caring, little one, but it's no use. Each day I find the darkness more comforting as it wraps around me. Maybe one day it will swallow me up."

Jumping to her feet, Oceana suddenly said, "Can I dance for you?"

Hema sighed. The last thing she wanted was a young child frolicking about, but she said, "All right."

Oceana spun around, barely missing the table in the center of the small room. Her poppy-red dress flared out and her dark ringlets bounced about her face. Watching the child spin wildly, Hema smiled.

When Oceana saw the smile on Hema's face, she stopped twirling. "Did I poke a hole in the black?"

Hema couldn't disappoint the girl. "A pinprick. Nothing more."

Oceana twirled a couple more times and then stopped in

front of Hema. She grabbed the woman's arm. "Let's go to the beach and watch the sunset. Maybe a sunbeam will get into the hole in your heart and the black will go away."

Hema yanked her arm back. "I'll never go near the beach and the treacherous sea again. My friends talked me into going the day we found you, but I will not go back. Looking at the ocean is like looking at a murderer." She fixed her eyes on Oceana's aquamarine gaze. "I will not change my mind. Don't ask me a second time."

"Can I go?"

Nodding, Hema said, "Of course. Be back before dark." She watched Oceana run down the dirt path toward the sea, her hair whipping around her face. She was a strange one. All cuddly and sweet like a little girl, yet in some ways, oddly grown-up. Hema didn't know what to make of Oceana. Already she had Hema pushing the black thoughts to the back of her mind for a few precious moments. But those moments were fleeting, and the black soon consumed her again.

Eating didn't interest Hema and she was now skin and bones because she had lost her desire for food when she'd lost her family. But she had to take care of Oceana for the month, so she began preparing supper.

With the girl gone, the blackness took over once again. It was an effort just to move around the small room to gather the food she needed to make the meal.

An hour later, Oceana came bursting into the dwelling. "I found something so pretty I had to bring it to you." Hema was standing against the wall in the dark. Oceana tugged at the woman's hand until she was in the center of the small room where light shone from the open doorway.

Oceana held out her hand. Lying on her palm was a seashell. "You can hear the ocean when you put it next to your ear. Listen."

Hema's legs began to tremble and she sat down, not taking the shell. "Why would I want to hear the sound of the sea that took my family?" she asked, shaking her head.

"I thought it would remind you of the times your children played on the beach."

Hema shuddered. "Take it away."

"Can I put it by my sleeping mat?"

"As long as you keep it out of my sight. I don't want any reminders of that day."

"But everything is a reminder of that day," Oceana said. "You can't hide from it."

"Yes I can. I can stay in the darkness."

For three days when she wasn't working, Hema sat in the dark room staring into space. Oceana tried to coax her outside.

"Please, Mama Two," Oceana begged, "come with me and sit in the sun. It will make you feel good." But Hema stubbornly shook her head.

Oceana made tea and brought it to the woman. "Please drink this," she coaxed. Hema shook her head and refused it. Oceana took the tea away and then sat down next to Hema. "I will stay with you in the dark," she said.

Several hours later, Hema looked over and saw Oceana sitting against the wall, fast asleep. She woke the child. "Go to bed, Oceana."

The girl rubbed her eyes. "No, I want to sit by you."

Hema smiled at Oceana's determination. "I'm going to lie down and sleep now. You should, too."

Oceana waited until Hema was on her mat. Then she curled up on her own.

The next week when Hema walked up the hill to do housekeeping at the tourist hotel, she thought about Oceana instead of her departed children. Was the little girl some sort of emissary? Hema laughed aloud at her fanciful thinking.

But she couldn't shake the feeling. Where had Oceana come from? And why? Once again she realized the blackness lifted, ever so slightly, when she thought of the girl.

Spotting several orphan children begging at the front of the hotel, Hema quickly darted around the building to the back door. She couldn't bear to see their empty eyes.

When Hema came home from work, Oceana was nowhere in sight. The seashell lay on her mat, half covered by her dresses. For a brief moment, Hema was tempted to pick it up and put it to her ear, but instead she turned away.

A few minutes later, Oceana came bounding into the dwelling. Hema was sitting in the dark. "I picked these for you," Oceana said, holding out a bouquet of white, yellow and pink wildflowers. She pulled out one of the white flowers and held it up. "Maybe this one will fit in the pinprick hole in your heart."

"I don't think so," Hema said brusquely. "The hole has closed up again."

The girl plopped down on the floor, still holding the wild-flowers. She laid them on her lap and scrunched up her face, hurt etched on her small features.

Seeing the expression on Oceana's face, Hema knelt beside the child. She took the bouquet. "The flowers are beautiful," she admitted. "Thank you."

Oceana's face brightened. "Do you really like them?"

"Yes. My little girl used to bring me flowers too. I miss her so much. I miss all of them."

Oceana scooted over to Hema and put her small arms around the woman's neck. "I won't bring you flowers any-more if it makes you sad."

Sniffing, Hema said, "I think flowers will make our place look nice." That wasn't what she had intended to say. She'd meant to tell Oceana never to bring flowers into the house again—that she couldn't bear the reminder. But somehow the words came out differently. Before she could retract them, Oceana's face beamed with pleasure and Hema just couldn't take that joy away from the girl.

Oceana hesitantly held up the white flower she'd tried to give Hema earlier. "If the hole in your heart closed up, you could put the flower in your hair instead."

Hema took the offering and slid the stem behind her ear. Then she took Oceana's face in her hands and kissed her forehead. "You are truly a very special little girl."

Oceana giggled. "I think a little happy snuck into your heart."

Several days later, after a lunch of soup, rice and crackers, Hema had to get to the hotel to clean the rooms of the vacating tourists. Instead of going directly up the path to the hotel, she detoured and walked on a ledge that overlooked the sea. At first she kept her eyes glued to the ground, afraid to look at the water. But she could hear the waves lapping at the shore and felt a tug in her heart. Shading her eyes from the glare of the afternoon sun, she slowly turned toward the ocean, her family's coffin.

The excruciating pain that pierced her heart almost made her double over. Her legs buckling, Hema fell to her knees. Then dropping her head in her hands, she wept for the loss of her beloved children and husband. When Hema finally raised her head, Oceana stood before her. The sun was behind the child, giving the illusion that she was aglow with a bright light. Hema squinted to reduce the blinding whiteness that surrounded the girl. When Oceana walked toward Hema, the brilliance faded.

"Come, Mama Two, I'll walk with you to the hotel." Oceana held her small hand out to the woman and laced their fingers together.

Neither the child nor the woman spoke as they walked up the hill. Hema looked down at Oceana's dark curly hair, the ringlets tousled by the breeze. With her free hand Hema smoothed the unruly strands of hair. Oceana looked up at her and smiled. She opened her mouth to say something, but Hema silenced her. "Don't speak. The stillness is soothing."

Oceana bent down and picked a bright blue wildflower. Holding it out to Hema, Oceana couldn't contain herself any longer and said, "I think another pinprick of happy snuck into your heart." She kicked up the sand with her bare feet and gave Hema a sidelong glance.

But Hema stared ahead, lost in memories. Suddenly she turned to Oceana, saw the flower and took it gently from her. "Would you like to spend the afternoon at the hotel? Other children come every day to beg from the tourists. Maybe you could play with them. Or just keep them company. They are lonely little people. Most of them have lost all their family, too."

"Oh, yes," replied Oceana. "I will be very kind to them."

When they reached the hotel, several little girls and boys were hanging around the front entrance. "I'll leave you here. I have to go in the back door," Hema said.

Ocean nodded and walked over to the other children who looked up at her with dark, sad eyes. Hema watched as Oceana's aquamarine eyes took in the situation. She had no doubt the child would work some sort of miracle with the little orphans.

"Let's pick wildflowers," she said to the other children. "I'll show you how to weave them into a crown and you can sell them to the tourist ladies." The sad eyes lit up and smiles spread across the brown faces. Hema smiled slightly and went into the hotel.

When her work was finished and she came out of the hotel,

Hema watched Oceana as she sat in the middle of the children. Dozens of wildflower crowns were spread out on the ground. "Did you sell any?" Hema asked.

The children laughed gleefully and held up coins and bills the tourists had paid them. They quickly went back to work on their project.

"Mama Two, I made a special one for you. Here, let me put it on you." Oceana stood up and held out a white crown made of jasmine petals.

All the children turned to watch, so Hema couldn't refuse. She knew that wearing the wildflowers would mean she had given up some of the darkness and wasn't sure she was ready. But she bent down in front of Oceana and the girl placed the wreath on her head.

Hema suddenly felt lightheaded and swayed. She blinked to clear her head as Oceana's blue-green eyes watched her intently, a white glow shining behind her. Hema blinked again and the light faded.

"I'm tired. Let's go home for supper." Hema began walking.

But Oceana tugged on her arm. "Can my friends come too?"

Hema's eyes widened. "All of them?"

"Who would we choose to leave behind?"

Sighing, Hema said, "Bring them, but just to eat. Then they have to leave."

Six children between the ages of four and seven followed Hema and Oceana. They all filed into Hema's house and the boys sat on the floor counting their money while the girls sat on Oceana's bed mat, taking turns listening to the sounds of the seashell.

They chatted during the meal, and Hema remembered the times when she ate with her family. She smiled and adjusted the crown on her head. Oceana watched her. "What is it?" Hema asked the girl.

"I think lots of pinpricks got into your heart today, letting in happy."

Hema didn't deny the girl's declaration. By opening herself to Oceana and the other children, she had allowed herself to slip out of the dark cocoon. Her heart somehow did seem fuller tonight. But she knew she'd retreat to the safety of the darkness as soon as the children left and Oceana fell asleep. And soon Oceana's month would be up.

The children didn't want to leave. "Please," they begged with large, soulful eyes. "We can sleep on the floor. We don't have a mama or a papa anymore." The littlest one leaned against Hema's knee. "I'll be good."

Hema's heart felt as if it were going to burst. She looked down at the little boy beside her. She felt needed again, a feeling she thought lost to her forever. "You can all stay if you behave yourselves and do as I say."

Six small heads nodded. Oceana smiled and her sea-green eyes sparkled. "I'll help you take care of them," she said. "The two littlest girls can sleep with me."

Before Hema knew what was happening, the children began moving things around to make room for the four who had to sleep on the floor.

The young boy climbed up on her lap, reached up and touched her face. "Can I sleep with you? My mama used to let me sleep with her sometimes."

Hema blinked back tears. She felt surrounded by a glow, as if the children were radiating warmth and brightness. Her heart felt full and this time she didn't question how long the feeling would last. It was enough that at the moment dark-ness was replaced with light, maybe even a small semblance of joy. She smiled down at the little boy on her lap. "I will make room for you on my mat."

The following week, after all the children were asleep, Hema walked over to Oceana's sleeping mat and tapped the girl on the shoulder. Rubbing her eyes, Oceana whispered, "What is it, Mama Two?"

"I want to go to the sea."

Oceana bolted upright and climbed carefully over the two girls asleep in her bed. "Do you want me to go with you?" Hema nodded.

The two tiptoed over the children sleeping on the floor and left the dwelling in silence. As they walked, the sound of the waves breaking on the shore grew louder. Neither of them spoke as they neared the ocean. The moon slipped from behind a cloud, a ray of soft light glimmered on the water. When they were close enough to feel the salt water spray their faces, Oceana tugged Hema's arm. The woman shook her head and sat down in the sand. Oceana dropped down beside her.

Hema stared at the ocean for a long time. "Are you sad, Mama Two?" Oceana asked.

"Yes and no." The woman turned to the girl. "I came here tonight to say good-bye to my children, to let them go." She picked up some sand and let it sift through her fingers. "I will never forget them, but I must let them go peacefully. I don't think they would want me to live in darkness."

"Does that mean you'll get more pinpricks in your heart?"

Hema didn't answer Oceana, but her mouth moved as if she were whispering to someone, maybe praying. After a long silence she turned to Oceana and smiled. "Let's go home to the children." Hema took Oceana's hand and swung it back and forth as they walked toward the dwelling.

"Are you going to keep the children?" Oceana asked as she fingered the tiny heart that hung from the chain around her neck.

Hema abruptly stopped walking. Of course. That was the answer. Oceana would be leaving soon and if Hema wanted happiness to fill her heart, she had to open it wide. She would embrace the children who now depended on her. Turning to Oceana, she smiled and said, "Yes, Oceana. I will be their mother."

Oceana clapped her hands gleefully. Peering at Hema, she asked, "Do you have another pinprick in your heart, Mama Two?"

Hema planted a kiss on top Oceana's curly head. "My heart has so many pinpricks, it's like a pincushion."

"And is happy sneaking in?"

Hema nodded and her smile lit up her face. "Happy, and light, and joy, too." Then, playfully she took Oceana's hands and spun her around and around.

When they were out of breath, Hema said, "Let's hurry home to the children."

Before they arrived at the small house, Hema turned to Oceana and said, "Thank you."

"For going to the sea with you?"

"No Oceana, for banishing the blackness by spreading your light." Hema thought of the children waiting for her and smiled. "For bringing joy back into my life."

Belief

Mama Three

Every morning without fail, Ushma stood in her doorway looking up at the sky to see if the sun had risen. She wouldn't take anyone's word for the dawning of a new day. She had to see the sunrise with her own eyes.

It was hard to fathom that before the killer wave had scraped her heart raw and left it torn and bleeding, Ushma had believed only in good. But now she didn't believe in anything. She was a skeptic, a disbeliever, always expecting the very worse that could happen. She had lost her faith in all the things she used to take for granted. That way, she thought she could protect her fragile heart and never be hurt again.

A gentle soul, known and loved for her sweet nature, Ushma wondered what it would be like to have a little girl in the house once more. She was sure it would bode ill. Her only child, a daughter, had been yanked from the arms of an uncle and sucked into the roiling sea, never to resurface.

Ushma wasn't sure she could tolerate comparing the two girls. But she had committed to taking Oceana for a month and would abide by her word.

Watching Oceana in a blue dress with pink flowers bordering the neckline skip up the dirt path toward her, Ushma shook her head. The girl's feet and legs were caked with dirt and her dress was covered in dust. "Wash before you come inside," she said to the girl when she reached the dwelling. The heart on the silver chain around Oceana's neck gleamed in the sunlight.

Oceana smiled and handed Ushma the poppy-red dress she carried in a bundle. "Would you hold my dress for me, please? I don't want to get it wet."

Ushma nodded and said, "Hurry. I have to leave for the hotel in a few minutes and I must talk to you before I go."

Using some old rags to dry off after splashing water on her legs, Oceana hurried into the dwelling. Ushma looked down at the girl's feet and rolled her eyes. Oceana followed her gaze and said, "Oops. I missed some of the dirt, didn't I?"

"No matter. Sit down and have some noodles." She felt a longing for her own daughter as she watched Oceana eat. "I think it might rain so you'd better stay inside while I'm at work."

Puzzled, Oceana looked up and said, "Rain? How can it rain? There aren't any clouds in the sky."

"Well, you just never know. Better to be safe in the house."

"But Mama Three, rain doesn't hurt. It feels good to get wet." She scrunched up her nose. "And it will clean my feet."

"Please, Oceana, stay inside. Something bad is bound to happen." Ushma wrung her hands.

Belief

Oceana leaned over and touched the woman's tense fingers. "Nothing bad is going to happen. Honest."

Ushma smiled sadly. "I wish I could believe you, but I don't believe in anything anymore."

"But, why Mama Three?" Oceana said, her hands still on the woman's.

Ushma turned her face away to hide her anguish. "I believed my little girl was safe with her uncle while I was working." Shaking her head, she said softly, "But she wasn't. She was whisked away by the killer wave, lost to me forever." Sighing, she turned back to gaze into Oceana's sea-green eyes. "So you see, there's nothing more to believe in."

Oceana stood up and went around the small table to stand at Ushma's side. "You could believe in me," she offered.

"Don't ask that of me, child. Please."

Leaning over, Oceana put her arms around Ushma's neck and kissed her cheek. "Okay. Can I go outside if I stay close to the house?" She quickly added, "The other Mamas let me."

Ushma hesitated, and then agreed. "All right, but don't go near the sea. It might snatch you away, too."

Days later as Ushma walked to the hotel she had a premonition that something terrible was going to happen. She hoped Oceana wasn't in danger. The day went by slowly. By the time her shift was finished, Ushma had worked herself into a frenzy and was sure when she got home she would find that some kind of tragedy had occurred. She hastened her steps knowing something horrible awaited her.

Oceana came running toward her and Ushma collapsed, her arms outstretched toward the girl. "What happened? Are you all right? Quick, tell me what's wrong," cried Ushma, her words coming out in a torrent.

"Nothing's wrong," Oceana reassured her, helping Ushma to her feet. "I just came to meet you."

"You're sure you're not keeping something from me?" She peered intently into Oceana's eyes that were wise beyond her tender years.

The girl shook her head. "Everything's okay. Nothing happened." She kept hold of Ushma's hand as they walked home. "You know, Mama Three, it's more fun to think good things than bad things."

Ushma halted her steps. "You don't understand. If I think bad things are going to happen and they don't, then I'm relieved. But if I think good things are going to happen and I get bad ones instead, then my world crashes down around me." She began walking again. Oceana skipped alongside her.

"But don't your insides hurt when you think bad things are going to happen?"

Ushma smiled down at Oceana. "Yes, but the relief I feel afterward makes up for it."

Oceana scrunched up her nose. "I think I like expecting good better than expecting bad."

"I did, too, at one time," Ushma said, biting her bottom lip. She touched Oceana's shoulder. "Tell me about your family, your mother. What was she like?"

Oceana looked puzzled. "You and the other Mamas are my mother."

"But before us. Before we found you adrift in the sea."

Oceana shook her head. "There was nothing before that."

"Of course there was," Ushma said, agitated.

"No there wasn't," Oceana insisted.

"So you just materialized out of thin air," she persisted.

"I don't know what that means." Oceana said softly, kicking up dust with her bare feet.

"You had to live somewhere before we found you."

Oceana turned to Ushma. "Why?"

Ushma said nothing, but shivered even though the afternoon sun warmed the air.

The next night, Ushma paced back and forth across the small room, wringing her hands. She stopped abruptly and peered out the doorway into the darkness. Her body shuddered as a feeling of gloom settled upon her.

"You have to learn to believe all over again, Mama Three," Oceana said.

Smiling weakly as she turned to the girl, Ushma said, "And you're going to teach me how?"

"No," Oceana answered spinning around and raising her hands out to her sides. "This is going to teach you."

"And what is *this* you speak of?"

"The earth, the sky, the sea. They will teach you to believe if you let them."

Intrigued by the child's strange beliefs, Ushma said, "And how do I let them?"

"They'll let you know when it's time."

Now Ushma laughed. *"They'll* let me know? And exactly how will *they* let me know?"

Oceana shrugged lightly. "I guess you'll just have to wait and see."

"Your imagination is running wild, child. What did the other Mamas think of your ranting like this?"

"They got used to it."

"So what should I believe in first?" Ushma asked condescendingly, still pacing.

Oceana seemed to ponder this question. "That nothing bad is going to happen tonight."

Ushma froze in her steps, unable to breathe. "Can you promise me that?"

Nodding, Oceana said, "I promise."

The following week after supper, Ushma sang to Oceana as they sat next to each other. Ushma ruffled Oceana's curly hair, but her frightened eyes kept darting to the doorway.

"What are you looking for?" Oceana asked.

"I'm wondering if the moon and the stars are out tonight," Ushma said as she hugged Oceana to her breast.

"What would happen if they weren't?"

"There would be no light. Everything would be black."

Oceana shrugged. "But the sun would come up tomorrow morning and make everything light again."

"Supposing the sun doesn't make an appearance tomorrow, or ever?"

Turning to Ushma, Oceana said, "Then we'll be stuck in blackness."

Ushma sucked in her breath.

"But," Oceana continued, "I believe the moon and the stars are out and the sun will shine."

She looked into Ushma's anxious eyes and waited. They sat in silence for several minutes. Then Ushma spoke. "If I let myself believe in good again, then I am telling my little girl that life without her is good, that the world without her is good, that each day without her is good. And that's a lie. So I must choose not to believe." She then turned to look into Oceana's eyes. "Can your young mind grasp what I mean, dear child?"

Oceana nodded. "But Mama Three, I don't think your daughter would want you to believe only in the bad things. She wouldn't want you to suffer like that."

A spark of comprehension shone in Ushma's eyes for a moment. Then they clouded over and she said, "This is all too new for me, too complicated. It's so much easier to believe in bad. I'm used to it now."

"But it must hurt," Oceana said.

Ushma nodded. "It's like losing her over and over again."

Suddenly, Oceana said, "Let's play a game of make-believe."

"Make-believe?"

Oceana nodded. "You can be Shiny Star and I'll be Yellow Sun."

Ushma threw her head back and laughed. "How do you get those ideas of yours?"

Shrugging, Oceana said, "I don't know. They just pop into my head." She peered into the woman's eyes. "Do you want to play?"

"I'm not sure what to do."

"Me neither. We'll just have to start and see what happens."

"Okay. You go first."

"Shiny Star, will I see you each night in the black sky?"

Ushma hesitated.

"It's make-believe, Mama Three," Oceana reminded the woman.

"Yes, Yellow Sun, I will hang in the sky for all to see."

"Promise, Shiny Star?"

Ushma nodded. "And Yellow Sun, will you brighten each day with your presence to warm us and give us light?"

"I promise to be there every day, even though some days clouds will keep you from seeing me."

Oceana and Ushma seemed to have settled into their role-playing. Then Oceana said, "And sometimes Shiny Star, the black clouds in your heart will keep you from seeing me. But I promise I will be there."

Drawing in a shaky breath, Ushma said softly, "Help me to believe in you, Yellow Sun."

"First you have to believe in yourself, Shiny Star."

For the next couple of weeks, Ushma silently played the game of make-believe whenever she was alone. She held purposeful conversations with Shiny Star and Yellow Sun. To her amazement, they answered her on some intuitive level. It wasn't that she heard voices, but something filled her with answers. Was this what Oceana meant when she said the earth, the sky and the sea would teach her to believe if she let them?

One day Ushma walked down to the beach and looked out at the vast ocean. Silently, she spoke. *Sea, what can you teach me about believing again?* With her eyes closed, Ushma waited, but the sea didn't answer. Disappointed, she looked around her and said, *Earth, what can you teach me about believing again?* But earth had no answers for her either. She turned around and walked home where Oceana was waiting for her.

"Oceana," she asked, "why do the stars and sun speak to me but not the sea and the earth?"

"I don't know. What do you think?"

Ushma pondered this question. "Is it because I have come to believe in the stars and sun?"

Oceana shrugged her small shoulders.

Her eyes widening, Ushma then answered her own question. "I think that's it. Not only do I believe in them, but I don't think bad things about them."

"The stars and sun are easy to believe in," Oceana said. "It's harder to believe in the earth and sea. But they will talk to you if you pay attention."

"Is this still make-believe?" Ushma asked with an embarrassed smile.

Oceana shook her head. "Believing is very real."

Ushma toyed with the braid that hung over her shoulder. "Tell me, what do you believe in?"

"I believe in you. And when you believe in yourself, the other kinds of believing will be easy."

"I don't know how to believe in myself again. I'm like a plate wiped clean," confessed the older woman.

"Every day," suggested Oceana, "remember one thing

you used to believe about yourself until your plate is filled up again."

Ushma looked puzzled. "You say you believe in me. What is there to believe?"

"Oh, many things, Mama Three. But what I believe doesn't matter. It's what you believe about yourself." Oceana took the woman's hands and led her to her mat. Sitting down, she patted the space next to her. "What's one thing you used to believe about yourself?"

Ushma sat down beside Oceana. "I used to have hope," she said softly.

Oceana bounced up and down on the mat, clapping her hands. "Hope. That's the first word for your plate."

After another week the plate was filled with words: hope, trust, strength, honesty, openness, love, kindness. Ushma decided it was time to talk aloud to the sea.

"Sea, can you promise never to hurt me again?" This time the sea spoke to her heart. "I understand, Sea," Ushma whispered, tears streaking her face. "It's not what I wanted to hear, but I understand."

Maybe the earth would have a different answer. So Ushma spread her arms wide and said, "Earth, can you promise never to hurt me again?" The earth spoke the same silent words to her heart as the sea.

That evening, Ushma called Oceana over to her mat. They sat on the edge side by side. "I filled up my plate as you suggested and then I talked to the sea and the earth today."

"Did they answer you?"

"Yes. They both said the same thing."

Oceana fidgeted, waiting for Ushma to continue. After several seconds of silence, the girl said, "Can you tell me what they said?"

Ushma nodded. "They told me there are no certainties in

life. How we face our challenges tests our spirits." She shook her head sadly. "It's not what I wanted to hear."

"What did you want to hear?"

"That the sea would remain calm, that the earth would stay whole, that there would be no more losses in my life."

Moving closer to Ushma, Oceana said, "I'm sorry."

The woman hugged Oceana to her side. "Don't be sorry. You have brought me much joy these past weeks and helped to heal my heart."

Oceana tapped Ushma on the knee. "Mama Three, what was your life like before me?"

Before you I was a lonely, desperate woman who wanted nothing more than to die, she said silently. *My heart was clamped shut and I was shriveling inside and out.*

"Everything was dark, Oceana, and you brought a ray of sunshine into my life. At first, the sun would only peek through the clouds. But in these past few days the clouds have disappeared and there is only light."

Oceana nodded as if she understood and was satisfied with the answer. Standing up, she twirled around and around.

That very night, Ushma's daughter came to her in a dream. They played on the beach and talked for a long while. "I must go now," her daughter said. She hugged her Mama tightly and began walking away. Turning back one last time, the little girl blew Ushma a kiss. "I love you, Mama," she whispered. And then the dream faded.

Ushma sat up in bed, her heart pounding wildly in her chest. She looked around expecting to see her daughter, but when she saw Oceana sleeping on her mat she realized she had been dreaming. *A most beautiful dream,* Ushma thought.

She slipped out of bed and shook Oceana's shoulder gently. "Wake up, dear child, I must talk to you."

Oceana rubbed her eyes with the backs of her hands.

Belief

"What is it? Is something wrong?"

Ushma smiled in the darkness and hugged this special girl to her breast. "I believe, Oceana. I believe in good, in beauty, in love. I believe in the sun, the stars and the sea. But most of all, Oceana, I believe that love doesn't die when a loved one passes—that love lives forever in our hearts."

And so Ushma and Oceana sat on the mat with their hands clasped as their belief in all things good wrapped around them like a soft, warm mantle.

Forgiveness

Mama Four

Gulika was sitting at her table when Oceana walked into the dwelling. Bitterness ebbed and flowed throughout Gulika's heart and soul, pinching her face into a constant scowl, aging her by ten years. Dry-eyed, she looked up at Oceana and managed a feeble smile.

"Mama Four, what's the matter? You look so sad."

"Of course I'm sad," Gulika snapped. "My two children are dead."

Oceana walked over to the distraught woman and smoothed her black hair. "The killer wave took many children…"

"But mine didn't have to die. It was my sister's fault. I'll never forgive her or forget what she did." Tears began to build up behind Gulika's eyelids. Her breath came in short gasps.

She forced herself not to pull her hair out and scream.

Oceana leaned closer to Gulika and hummed a well-known melody until the tense woman quieted. Then Oceana whispered, "Would you like me to braid your hair? I'm just learning and I need practice."

Gulika smiled woodenly and nodded. Oceana separated the woman's thick hair into three sections and wove one long braid that hung down Gulika's back. The child found a small purple ribbon and tied it around the end of the braid. "Did I fix you?" she asked, peering into Gulika's face.

Gulika shook her head. "I'm unfixable. How can you fix something when major parts are missing?"

"But for a couple of minutes you were fixed."

"What's a couple of minutes out of a lifetime?" She sat up straighter in the chair. "Be a good girl and go outside and play now."

Oceana shook her head. "Then you'll be alone and feel sorry for yourself."

"I've been alone for months now. And I'll be alone for the rest of my life. You can't change that, so go out and play." Oceana walked slowly to the door and then stopped and turned back to look again at Gulika. "Go," the woman said, pointing to the door.

After Oceana left the dwelling, Gulika threw herself across her cot and banged her fists against the thin mattress. "Where have you gone, my dear, sweet children?" she wailed. "I had so many plans for you. Without you I have nothing except bitterness in my heart." She closed her eyes tightly to hold back the flood of tears straining to be released.

The pain was deep and crushing. It was with her day and night, awake and sleeping. There were days when she would crouch in the middle of her small house and scream until her throat burned raw. But nothing could change what had happened that ill-fated day. And each day since then, her heart hardened more and more.

She didn't know how long she lay there when she felt a presence close by. Expecting to see her despised sister, she sat up quickly in readiness to vent her feelings once more. But it was Oceana. The girl looked as if she were on the verge of tears. "What wrong?" Gulika asked, getting to her feet. "Is something bad going on out there?" She pointed to the doorway.

Oceana shook her head. "Nothing's wrong. I'm just sad because you're sad." The girl swiped at a tear that ran down her dusty face. "Your pain bursts out of you and flies all over the place."

"What's that to you?" Gulika asked.

"It hurts whoever's near you." She sat down on the dirt floor. "Will you tell me about your pain?" Oceana looked up at Gulika with her tear-brimmed aquamarine eyes.

"I have to go to work now. Maybe I'll tell you another time." She turned her back on the girl and muttered as she walked away, "Why in the world would a child want to hear about someone's heartache?" She arched her eyebrows. "It must seem like a fairy tale to her, only this one doesn't have a happy ending."

A week went by, but like every day since the killer wave devoured her family, Gulika was consumed with hatred for her sister. It was the force that fueled her. She needed it to survive. She whipped through her tasks in record time at the hotel and was able to help her other women friends with their "to do" lists. In between Gulika's duties, her thoughts returned to Oceana and the child's request to hear about the woman's pain. There was no way she could sugarcoat it into a fairy tale even though her sister was worse than all the wicked witches ever written about.

Gulika's heart thumped against her chest and a sharp pain ripped through her stomach. She stopped her chore and took several deep breaths. Hatred was slowly eating away her insides. But she didn't care. She was never going to give up her hatred. Never.

A few nights later after a meager supper of rice and bread, Oceana sat at Gulika's feet. She looked up at the woman and asked, "Are you ready now?"

"Ready for what?" Gulika asked, even though she knew in her heart what the girl was waiting for.

"To tell your story," Oceana said simply.

Suddenly Gulika put her head in her hands. "I can't relive that day again. I can't."

"But you do. All the time. Your sad face shows it."

"My story is no fairy tale. It's a story of betrayal." She covered her face again. "Oh, I can't go on with this."

Oceana waited a few moments and then touched Gulika's head with her small hand and kept it there. "Maybe if you hear your story, it won't be as bad as you think it is."

Gulika's head jerked upright. "Are you saying I'm imagining things?" She glared at Oceana.

Oceana shook her head, dropping her hand to her side. "Sometimes when we think about things too much they get bigger than they really are."

Was Gulika really having this conversation with a child? She had to control herself or she would surely go over the edge and fall into oblivion. But would that be so bad? She noticed Oceana watching her, the girl's wise, blue-green eyes changing moment by moment. Suddenly, Gulika came to a decision. She stared straight ahead, then began speaking.

"My life was full and happy even though my husband had left us years ago. My children were healthy and I had a job that paid for food and clothes." She bit down on her lip.

"I was very close to my younger sister. I trusted her like no other. She took care of my children while I worked at the tourist hotel.

"The other Mamas and I were working the same shift the morning of the killer wave. We didn't know anything at first. When we heard screaming, we ran out of the hotel to see the fury of the ocean almost at the hotel's entrance. At first we didn't comprehend what it meant. Then we heard wailing from down below. Horrible, excruciating painful sounds. We all had the same thought. Our children. Our families. But by then the sea had pulled thousands of people into its belly. We made our way as close to the beach as we could get. Children and adults were spread out on the sand, all of them dead. Debris all around. Pieces of houses. Furniture scattered among the bodies. Huge trees bent and broken.

"I shouted for my sister and my children. But it wasn't until hours later that I found her." Gulika shook her head. Tears streamed down her face. Oceana put her small arms around the woman and leaned her cheek against Gulika's. Using the hem of her poppy-red dress, she wiped away the woman's tears.

"She was huddled in the corner of a makeshift shelter. Her children crouched next to her. 'Where are my children?' I screamed over and over, looking all around the room, trying to find them.

"My sister looked up at me, her dark eyes dull and lifeless. 'They're gone.'

"'What do you mean, they're gone?' I asked her dumbly. I couldn't understand what was happening.

"'There were too many. I couldn't save all of them. I only had two hands, two arms. They were washed away. I'm sorry, so sorry.'

"I looked at my two nephews huddled next to their mother.

I hated them for taking my children's place. I hated my sister for choosing her children over mine. I hated myself for being at work and not with them. I still hate my nephews. I still hate my sister. And I still hate myself."

Gulika looked at Oceana. "She let my children die."

"It wasn't her fault."

"Whose fault was it?"

Oceana shrugged. "Who would you hate if your sister and her children had died with yours?"

Gulika stared at Oceana for several seconds. Then she said, "But they didn't."

"That's not an answer."

"It's all the answer you're getting." Gulika rubbed her temples. "I'm finished talking. Go to bed."

Before Gulika left for work two weeks after Oceana's arrival, the child said, "We are all connected."

"And what exactly does that mean?" Gulika asked, her hands on her hips.

"We are one and you can't separate yourself."

"Did the other Mamas put that nonsense in your head?"

Oceana looked puzzled. "I don't think it's nonsense, but I'm not sure. Sometimes thoughts just come to me."

Gulika shook her head and left the dwelling without responding. Preoccupied, she didn't see her sister until she moved in step with Gulika. "Please, sister, talk to me. My heart is heavy with the burden of your hatred for me. I tried. I swear I tried…"

"I don't want to hear your excuses. Leave me alone." Gulika brushed away her sister's outstretched hand and glared at her. "You have your children. Go home to them."

"I need you. You are the only family I have."

"I'm not your family."

Gulika's sister put her hand to her mouth, her dark eyes

wide with grief. She backed away and then turned and ran in the opposite direction.

All day long, the question tormented Gulika: *Who would you hate if your sister and her children had died with yours?* Stamping her foot in exasperation Gulika wondered why she was paying attention to the words of a mere child. Yet the taunting words stayed with her.

Who would she hate? Who would she blame? Herself, of course. But in time she would be able to acknowledge that she was where she was meant to be that day. So then who would she hate? Who would she blame?

Nobody.

Gulika had to think about this in greater depth. It wasn't something she could accept immediately. Maybe never. Had she been in error blaming her sister? She shuddered. Her stomach churned and her heart beat faster and she clung to the hatred. If she let it go, she was afraid there would be nothing left of her.

A week later, instead of going home, Gulika made a detour. She walked in the direction of her sister's hut. She wasn't sure why, but she felt compelled to go that way. As she neared the dwelling, her heart picked up speed and she struggled for breath. What was she doing here? What craziness propelled her? She turned and ran all the way home.

When Gulika burst into her house, Oceana looked up, startled. "Is someone chasing you?" she asked the panting woman.

Gulika shook her head, clutching her stomach, taking in deep breaths. *Only my demons,* she said silently.

Wetting a rag, Oceana wiped Gulika's ashen face. When she lifted her head and looked into the child's eyes, Gulika was captivated by their inner glow. Light from the afternoon sun fell on Oceana's young shoulders, bathing her in radiance.

When Oceana said, "Did you see your sister today?" Gulika sucked in her breath.

"How did you know?"

"She came by this morning right after you left for work. She wanted to talk to you."

Gulika let out a sigh of relief and gathering her wits said, "I met her on the path, but we didn't talk."

"Why?"

"I have nothing to say to her except words of blame."

"She looked so sad this morning." Oceana ran her hand down Gulika's arm.

The woman felt her insides blazing. "What does she have to be sad about? She still has her children." She pulled away from Oceana's touch.

"I think she misses you."

"I miss my children, and if I can't have them, she can't have me."

"That's cruel, Mama Four."

Gulika burst into tears. "I know, but I can't help myself."

"Yes, you can," Oceana said, smoothing the woman's hair back from her face.

"Why do you torment me like this?"

"But, Mama Four, I'm not. You are."

Gulika laughed, a sound bordering on hysteria. "And do I just forget what happened to my children?"

Oceana shook her head slowly, the light still resting on her shoulders. "You let the wound heal."

"And exactly how do I do that?"

"By forgiving."

"Never!" Gulika shouted, standing up. "Never!"

"You know Mama Four, the killer wave didn't only take your children. It took you. It took your sister. And it took your nephews. It wiped out everyone in your family."

That night Gulika couldn't sleep. Oceana's words played over and over in her mind. The woman had to admit the child was right about the killer wave taking her whole family. They were nothing but empty shells wandering aimlessly. As empty as the shells left behind when the treacherous wave receded.

But could she forgive her sister? Gulika turned her head toward the wall and wept quietly.

At sunrise the next morning, Gulika walked to the market. She spotted her sister by a produce stand, her two boys tugging on her skirt. Gulika hid behind a mound of flowers and studied her sister's sad face. She glanced down at the faces of her nephews. Three empty shells. Four, if she counted herself. Did she want to be an empty shell for the rest of her life? Did she have a choice?

Oceana seemed to think she did. But what does she know about life? *Who would you hate if your sister and her children had died with yours?* Had Gulika been wrong these past months in blaming her sister? She shivered even though the day was balmy and the sun warmed her body.

All day at work Gulika couldn't get the agonizing image of her sister and her nephews out of her mind. She realized she had compounded the tragedy of losing her children by blaming her sibling. Because she knew in her heart that if she had been in her sister's place and unable to save all the children, she would have made the same choice and saved her own.

It was Oceana's last week when Gulika came to a decision that wrenched her insides. But she knew it was the right one, the only one. She hurried home to get Oceana. The child was standing in the doorway waiting. Her face and hands were clean and she wore her poppy-red dress.

"Come with me," Gulika said, reaching for the girl's outstretched hand. It didn't go unnoticed that Oceana never asked where they were going. Gulika had a strong inkling the child already knew.

"Shouldn't we stop at the market and buy some flowers?" Oceana asked, touching the heart dangling from the chain around her neck.

Gulika studied the upturned face of the astute child standing next to her. "Of course. And some sweets." After their purchases, Gulika put the sweets in her pocket and led the way up the path she knew as well as her own.

The sun was beginning to set and the woman stopped and looked out at the sea. She hesitated just long enough to gaze at the empty shells scattered on the sandy shore. The workers at the tourist hotel had cleared a portion of the beach soon after the killer wave had struck. Then, with a spring to her step Gulika continued walking, Oceana by her side.

When they approached a small hut, a young woman came to the doorway shading her eyes from the final glare of the day's sun. She stared at Gulika and Oceana as they drew near.

Tears streamed from the eyes of both women. Gulika crumpled to her knees and held out the bouquet of yellow and white flowers. "Sister, I have come to beg your forgiveness."

Gulika's sister sucked in her breath. Her hand flew to her mouth. Then she knelt in front of Gulika. The two women searched each other's faces and then clung to one another in a fierce embrace.

Oceana smiled and gently picked up the crushed flowers.

Gratitude

Mama Five

Madhur and Oceana were seated at a table the hotel manager had given the woman when the tourist hotel had been forced to replace several pieces of damaged furniture. They were sharing tea and crackers. Oceana looked around the room. "You have a lot to be thankful for," she said.

Madhur grunted and leaned across the table, her wrinkled face inches from Oceana. "Tell me one thing I should be grateful for." Not waiting for an answer from the child, Madhur continued. "I'm old, I need a cane to walk, most of my teeth have fallen out, and I've outlived all of my children." That despicable killer wave had seen to that and crushed her heart beyond repair. She looked at Oceana with rheumy eyes. "Everything I have or get, I deserve," she announced, banging her cane on the dirt floor for emphasis. Madhur looked down at the silver bracelet set with ruby chips encircling her wrist. A rich tourist had given it to her as a tip years ago. She never took it off.

Oceana opened her mouth to speak and Madhur pointed a bony finger at her. "I'm called the ancient one because I'm the oldest woman in the village, so don't talk back to me. I expect respect from you the same way I expect it from everyone else."

"Forgive me, Mama Five, but I think people are supposed to earn respect."

"So you're a little know-it-all. And how did you come by all this wisdom, young woman?"

"I'm not a woman. I'm a little girl."

Madhur raised her hands in mock-surrender. "Just a figure of speech." She continued to peer at Oceana over the table.

"I listened to the Mamas and learned from them."

"And did they tell you I needed to earn respect?"

"Nooo," Oceana answered, dragging out the word. "We never talked about the other Mamas."

Sitting back in her chair, Madhur said, "To get back to my question: what do you think I should be grateful for? What should any of us in this godforsaken place be thankful for?" Again she didn't wait for an answer but continued, "And what about you? What do you have to be thankful for? You don't even know where you came from or who you belong to."

Oceana smiled sweetly. At that moment a shaft of light fell on her face, illuminating the intensity of her aquamarine colored eyes. The silver chain and heart around her neck glimmered. She lowered her gaze to her hands.

Madhur leaned across the table. "Are you harboring secrets?"

When Oceana looked up again she was no longer in the ray of light. "I don't know what *harboring* means."

"Enough of this drivel. Here's some money. Go to the market and buy a bag of rice. Don't let them cheat you. I'd go myself but my hips ache." She stood up and hobbled over to one of the two cots the hotel manager had also given her. Dropping the cane to the side, she sat down gingerly.

When Oceana returned with the rice an hour later, she handed Madhur a bunch of wildflowers she had picked on the way home.

"What are these for?" Madhur asked curtly, glancing down at the flowers.

"They're for you."

"And what am I supposed to do with them?" She guessed the girl was trying to be nice to her because she wanted something. "If you're looking for a reward or a pat on the back, you won't get it from me." Over the years while working at the hotel, Madhur had picked up the selfish ways of some of the foreign tourists.

"I didn't expect anything, except maybe a smile or a thank you." The girl looked crestfallen.

"Huh!" Madhur bellowed. "You'll get no thanks from me." She dropped the flowers to the floor. "These are weeds."

Oceana picked up the flowers and touching their soft petals, placed them on the cot next to her poppy-red dress.

"Don't just stand there. Help me up, girl. I have to put the rice away." Her whole body ached with stiffness.

Oceana hurried to Madhur's side. Lifting up the heavy wood-carved cane, she handed it to the old woman. "Can I help you with the rice?"

"When I want your help I'll ask for it." Madhur hobbled over to the table. "Pick up the leaves you dropped from those weeds. I keep my place neat."

Oceana did as she was told. Then she asked, "Can we play a game after supper?"

"A game! I'm too old to play games."

"No you're not. And it's an easy one." Oceana looked up at Madhur with anticipation.

Madhur heaved a heavy sigh. She had nothing else to do after she cleaned up the dishes, so why not indulge this girl from nowhere for a spell? Truthfully, she had been feeling lonely the last few weeks and had looked forward to having Oceana stay with her. Although she would never admit that to anyone. She had the reputation for being hard so she had to be careful not to appear soft to the girl.

"You think I'm so old I can only play easy games?"

"No, Mama Five. I just thought you might like an easy game because you work hard all day in the house."

"I worked harder before the hotel let me go. They gave me some old furniture and thought that would make me happy. Then they had the nerve to say I was grumpy and rude to the tourists. Can you believe that?"

Oceana hid a smile behind her hand. "They didn't really know you or they never would have said that."

"And you know me? After a couple of hours in my house? I don't think so."

"I know you," Oceana said and walked over to her cot and sat down. "Tell me when you're ready to play."

"And what if I don't want to play?" Madhur snapped.

"That's okay. I'll wait until you do."

"You'll have a long wait," Madhur mumbled, waving her arms so the silver and ruby bracelet sparkled in the light.

"Can I try on your bracelet?" Oceana asked, her blue-green eyes large and round.

Madhur grumbled. "For a minute." She slipped the bracelet on Oceana's thin wrist. The bracelet was too large and fell to the floor. Madhur picked it up and tried to fasten it on her own arm again. "Help me, girl. Don't just stand there."

Oceana ran her fingers over the tiny rubies. "It's very pretty," she said, before closing the clasp.

After supper Madhur said, "What is this game you want to play?"

"I made it up. It's called *"Count Your Blessings."*

"The game's over. I don't have any blessings." Madhur watched Oceana carefully, wondering how the girl would respond to that.

"Oh, it's not over, Mama Five. We haven't even started yet. I'll go first so you can see how it's played."

"I told you I don't have any blessings to count! Didn't you understand me?" She leaned menacingly over Oceana.

"I did understand you, Mama Five, but this is a game. If you don't have a blessing, you make one up."

Madhur dropped her cane and sat down at the table across from Oceana. "As long as you know that these so-called blessings of mine are not real—they're imaginary."

"There's a little more to the game. You have to tell why the blessing is a blessing. But let me go first," she added before Madhur could disagree.

"Go ahead. I'm curious to hear what you consider a blessing."

"My poppy-red dress. When I wear it I feel special—even though it's fading from the sun—because Mama One made it for me." She nodded to Madhur. "Your turn."

The woman thought for a few seconds. "My cane. It helps me walk."

Oceana didn't comment. "My tears. They wash the dust out of my eyes."

"My bed. It welcomes my weary bones."

Oceana smiled. "The seven Mamas. For taking care of me."

Madhur's mouth curved up slightly, not quite a smile. "My

house. It shelters me."

"The rain. It makes the flowers grow."

Madhur held up her hands. "Enough. I'm tired of this game. I'm going to sleep."

Sometime during the night several days later, Oceana heard a thump and jumped out of bed. As she rushed to Madhur's cot, she tripped over the woman sprawled out on an old rug covering part of the dirt floor. Oceana bent down. "Mama Five, what happened? Are you all right?"

"If I was all right I wouldn't be on the floor. I stumbled and fell, and I can't get up."

Oceana tried with all her might to lift the woman but she couldn't budge her. The girl sat back on her haunches. Madhur reached down and cried out, "I can't feel my legs. They're gone."

"They're not gone, Mama Five. Maybe the fall made them numb."

But Madhur wasn't listening. "They're gone. I have no legs," she screamed. "How will I get around? Oh, what will I do?" she wailed, thrashing from side to side on the floor.

Oceana knelt down beside the woman and held her arms. "You must calm down. Think good thoughts. Breathe deeply."

Madhur snapped to attention and brushed away Oceana's hands. "Stop that nonsensical talk. Just go get someone to help me to bed."

"I'll be back as soon as I can." The girl threw on her dress and ran out of the dwelling.

Horrible thoughts ran through Madhur's head about never being able to walk again. She twisted and squirmed but no matter what she did, she couldn't get to a sitting position. All she accomplished was to push the rug into a heap.

This would never do. Madhur never offered help to anyone and she never asked for it for herself. She liked being left alone. But she couldn't stay on the floor. As hard as it was to admit, she needed help.

Where was that girl? What was she doing dilly-dallying? Why wasn't she back here with help? Madhur beat her fists on the dirt floor until she felt her flesh scraped raw. Unbidden tears came to her eyes. She hadn't cried in years—not even when she found out the killer wave had stolen her adult children. She had always been self-sufficient. She had never relied on anyone. She'd rather die than be at someone else's mercy.

Shaking her head, Madhur admitted to herself she was old, but she wasn't ready to die yet. She'd beat that girl silly when she got her hands on her. Who was she kidding? She might never walk again. The game, *Count Your Blessings,* came to mind. Her legs had been a blessing but she had taken them for granted. What else in life had she taken for granted? Now she was spouting gibberish like Oceana. She let out a stream of curses just as the girl and three women entered the house.

"Don't trip over me," Madhur called out. "We don't need more people sprawled on the floor."

Oceana giggled. "I'm glad you're okay, Mama Five."

Only she wasn't okay. She hadn't been okay for many years. Somehow all the goodness and kindness she'd embodied had drained from her drop by drop and left her a papery thin old hag.

"Stop standing around," Madhur ordered, "and somebody help me up."

The three women and Oceana grasped Madhur under the arms and legs and were able to pick her up and place her on the cot. "Some of you can go now," she said ungraciously. "I don't need a crowd hanging around."

The three friends huddled in a corner of the room. When

they turned around, Kamalika said, "We're not leaving until we're sure you're not seriously hurt. Then we'll take turns cooking and cleaning until you are able once again."

Mumbling, Madhur raised herself up on her elbows. "Go home now. Come back tomorrow if you must."

"It's already tomorrow," said Oceana. "The sun is rising on a new day."

Madhur snickered. "A poet. Do something useful and get me water. I'm thirsty."

Jasmira poured water into an old jelly jar and handed it to Madhur. "Try to sleep," she said.

"Sleep? With a house full of strangers?"

"We're not strangers. We're your friends."

Oceana sat down at the foot of Madhur's cot and tweaked the woman's toes. "Did you feel anything?"

Madhur's eyes opened wide. "I did! I did!" She turned to Oceana. "When we play your silly game again, I'll be able to honestly say I'm thankful for my toes." She sat up and rubbed her numb calves.

After a week in bed, Madhur was getting antsy. Suddenly her legs began to tingle. "I feel life coming back," she cried out. She swung her legs over the side of the bed. "Help me up. I want to walk. Girl, get my cane." But when she leaned on the cane and put weight on her legs she crumpled to the floor.

Oceana and Ushma rushed to the older woman. Once again they hoisted her by the arms and legs and laid her on the cot. Madhur turned her head to the bare wall, for once not uttering a sarcastic remark.

Oceana sat down on the cot next to Madhur. "You weren't ready yet," she said. Madhur didn't answer. "You need two helpers, one on either side to walk with you until you're stronger." Still Madhur didn't answer.

Gratitude

"We can try again later in the day," said Ushma, watching Oceana and Madhur.

Suddenly Madhur turned in her narrow bed. "Get out!" she shouted, pointing to the doorway. When Ushma shook her head, Madhur yelled, "I don't need you or want you here."

"Yes you do, Mama Five," Oceana said, rubbing the woman's legs. "Deep inside, you really want her to stay. I'm too little to help you get around. You need the other Mamas taking turns." She leaned down and whispered in the woman's ear, "Can't you find it in your heart to be grateful and say thank you?"

Madhur stubbornly shook her head. "I am the ancient one of the village; it's their duty to take care of me."

"No it's not. They are all grieving their lost children. Their only duty is to take care of themselves. They want to take care of you because they love you, not because they have to."

"What's the difference?" Madhur asked, turning to Oceana.

Oceana shook her head. "Why can't you say the words: *thank you?* They're simple words. What makes it so hard for you?"

"Leave it. If she wants to stay, let her. I'm going to sleep now." Madhur turned her back on Ushma and Oceana.

Another week passed. Dark shadows were creeping into the dwelling when Madhur awoke. She called Oceana to her side. "Sit here," she said. "I want to tell you a story.

"I had an identical twin sister. But our personalities were totally different. I was kind and goodhearted and grateful for any morsel thrown to me. She was self-centered and a controller. Through all the years of our growing up, I never once saw her cry. She was tough skinned while I was thin skinned. My emotions were always close to the surface. She didn't have any.

"Despite our differences, I idolized her. And true to form,

69

she took advantage of me. I was always at her beck and call. Whenever she deemed me worthy of her smile, my heart would fill to overflowing with love and gratitude. I must have thanked her thousands of times during our growing up years. She never once thanked me.

"She married the man I loved. She lived the life I wanted. Seeing this made me realize you didn't get anything by being grateful. The way to get what you wanted was to take control and expect to have things done for you.

"So that's what I do. Now stop asking me to thank these women when in fact they are here because they want to be, not because I asked them."

"Was your sister happy, Mama Five?" Oceana asked.

Madhur hesitated. "No. She died alone. I had washed my hands of her by that time."

"Yet you say you want to be like her."

"Yes, but…"

"Are you happy, Mama Five?"

The woman covered her face with her hands and wept. Oceana sat down and put her small arms around Madhur. "Are you?" the girl asked again.

"I'm miserable. I've been miserable most of my life."

"Then maybe it's time to let the little girl in you come back again as the kind, goodhearted, grateful person you once were."

"It's too late."

"It's never too late."

Over the next few weeks, the women took turns ministering to Madhur. They weren't thanked, but neither were they insulted. Madhur still couldn't walk on her own and spent most of her waking hours thinking about her conversation with Oceana. The girl had said it was never too late. But what did a child know when it came to the mind and needs of an ancient one?

Did she want to die alone the way her twin had? Madhur shuddered. Truth be told, she welcomed the comings and goings of her three friends and the girl. She enjoyed their company and secretly wondered if that was why she couldn't walk on her own. Was she keeping herself an invalid so they wouldn't leave her?

Madhur silently said the words *thank you* over and over, but she couldn't get herself to say them aloud. Even so, her friends cheerfully cooked for her, helped her get around, and cleaned the dwelling daily. Madhur was acutely aware that they did these chores for her out of the goodness of their hearts, not expecting anything in return. She felt her heart softening toward them.

It came to her on Oceana's last night. Madhur bolted upright to a sitting position, amazed at the discovery. She was loved. And she was grateful for that love. She smiled in the darkness.

Using her cane she nudged Oceana, who had moved her cot closer to Madhur's after her fall. "Wake up, child."

"Is something wrong?" Oceana asked, rubbing her eyes.

"No. I want to play *Count Your Blessings.*"

"Now? In the middle of the night?" Oceana was at once wide awake.

"Yes, now. Scoot over by me. I'll go first."

Oceana did as she was told and sat at the foot of the cot, hugging her knees to her chest.

Madhur sighed contentedly. "I have many blessings." She smiled and then continued, "First, all my friends. They love me despite my ornery disposition." She placed her bony hand on Oceana's curly head. "And especially you, dear child, for helping me realize my many blessings even though I had chosen a narrow, self-centered life.

"Because of you, I will spend my last years grateful for the beauty that surrounds me, for the loving people who take care of me, and for the child who awakened me from a delusional sleep." She gently pulled one of Oceana's curls just as the girl opened her mouth to ask a question. "I have something for you."

"For me?" Oceana asked, touching her chest.

"Yes. Put your foot up on my knee." Oceana did as she was told. Madhur closed her eyes and hesitated. Then she slipped the bracelet off her arm and fastened it around Oceana's ankle. She leaned back and admired it on the young girl.

"An anklet," Oceana exclaimed. "It matches my red dress." She jumped up and twirled around, her dark ringlets flying across her face. She stopped abruptly and looked into Madhur's eyes. "But you love it so much. How can you bear to give it away?"

Madhur took Oceana in her arms and hugged the child against her breast. "It's a token of my gratitude for your helping me." She nudged Oceana gently. "Now go back to bed."

Oceana smiled and padded over to her cot. She closed her sea-green eyes but before sleep overtook her Madhur called out, "You were right. They are simple words. I kind of like the way they roll off my tongue."

And Madhur whispered, "Thank you."

Acceptance

Mama Six

Jasmira walked hurriedly up the path to her dwelling. She spotted Oceana sitting on the ground, her poppy-red dress spread out around her. Looking bored, the child twirled her anklet around and around. "Oh, Oceana, I'm so sorry I'm late," Jasmira said, out of breath. "I was down at the beach calling my children to come home for supper."

Oceana held her extra dress rolled up into a ball and stood to greet the woman. "But Mama Six, your children are gone. The killer wave…"

"Don't be silly," Jasmira interrupted, flapping her hands, "they're just off playing somewhere. They'll be home soon. Come inside. I'll show you where you'll sleep." Oceana shrugged and followed Jasmira.

Four sleeping mats almost filled the small one-room dwelling. "My two boys sleep on that one," Jasmira said, pointing to the mat farthest from the door, "and my daughter sleeps there." She pointed to another. "This one is mine," she said, indicating a mat by the stacked wood that served as a table. "And that one is yours." She pointed to a small mat against the side wall.

Oceana placed her extra dress on her mat and sat down. She studied the woman puttering around the room making tea and placing crackers on the table. "How old are your children?" she asked, watching Jasmira's face.

"The boys are twins. They're six. The girl is eight." She smiled at Oceana. "They're nice children. You'll have fun with them. It won't be so lonely for you while I'm working."

Taking a deep breath, Oceana said, "But the other Mamas told me all of you had lost your children to the killer wave. I don't understand."

"They made a mistake, child. My three children are alive and well. They have to be. They should be home soon, although sometimes they stay out all night. But I don't worry about them. They'll show up sometime."

"Are you playing make-believe, Mama Six?"

"Whatever are you talking about?" She glared at Oceana. "I told you my children are fine. Don't try to change that, you hear? And there's no need to question what I say."

"I didn't mean to make you mad. I just wanted to know."

Jasmira sighed. "I'm not angry. They'll show up. You'll see." She busied herself in the small room fixing supper. Five cracked plates were placed on the table. Oceana shivered and Jasmira asked, "Are you cold?"

Oceana stared at the empty plates. "No, I'm okay."

"We'll eat without them," Jasmira said. "No sense in waiting. Pull your mat over and sit down there." She pointed to the space across from her. Oceana obediently followed orders.

"Where do they go when they stay out all night?" Oceana asked, unable to take her eyes off the empty plates.

"With friends. Or they sleep on the beach. They like being outside." Jasmira chewed on her fingernail. "When the killer wave swept away most of the children of the village, my three were playing a game of hide and seek."

"Hide and seek?"

Jasmira nodded. "They hid from the killer wave and were saved."

Oceana stood up and walked around the small table to stand at Jasmira's side. "Did you see them after the killer wave came?" she asked softly.

Jasmira's hands fidgeted on the tabletop. She moved the crackers around and picked up the bowl of rice. She stared straight ahead.

"Did you, Mama Six?" Oceana persisted.

"No! No, I didn't. But I know they're all right and that soon they'll come back home." She looked at Oceana. "They're probably still hiding," she said, while her throat constricted with fear.

Oceana put her arms around Jasmira's neck and rested her cheek on the woman's. "I don't think they're hiding."

Nudging Oceana away from her, Jasmira said, "What do you know? You're only a child." She moved the rice to the other side of the table. Then her mood abruptly changed and she smiled at Oceana. "Do you like playing hide and seek?"

Oceana nodded and waited.

"Good. We'll go to the beach in a little while and maybe you'll be able to help me find my children's hiding place."

Jasmira and Oceana spent an hour on the beach searching behind rocks, under brush, beneath debris left by the brutal force of the killer wave. But Jasmira's children weren't there.

"Can we go home now?" Oceana asked. Her ringlets, plumped up by the damp sea breeze, bounced around her face.

"Just a little longer. I know they're here somewhere." Jasmira looked around frantically and shouted their names.

Silence was her answer.

"They must be with their friends. Let's go home." Jasmira hummed to herself as she walked briskly back to the dwelling, Oceana skipping to keep up. Inside the house, Jasmira's mood changed again. "I miss them," she said. She desperately clung to the hope that she'd see them again.

Oceana didn't have to ask whom she meant. "Mama Six, have you talked to the other Mamas about your children?"

"I try, but they won't listen. They keep telling me the killer wave found their hiding place and swept them into the sea." Her dark eyes misted and she pushed back the tendrils that had come loose from her bun and stuck to her cheeks.

"Maybe that's what happened and why you haven't seen them." Oceana looked intensely into Jasmira's sad eyes. She reached over and placed her hand on the woman's shoulder.

Jasmira shook her head vehemently. "No, they're out there someplace. I couldn't survive another day if what you say is true."

"But…"

"No more talk. I'm tired. It's always so exhausting looking for them. And when I can't find them, the letdown is as painful as a sharp stick piercing my heart."

"Do you want me to sing for you?" Oceana asked.

Jasmira rubbed her forehead and sat down on a stool. "That might be soothing." So Oceana sang one of the nursery songs she knew. When she finished, Jasmira said, "Sit here by my side and we'll sing a song together."

Oceana quickly scooted over to Jasmira. "Did you and your children sing together?"

Nodding, Jasmira said, "Every night. I miss the time we
spent together after supper. It was relaxing after working long
hours. We'd sing and tell stories. They loved hearing about
the crazy things the tourists did at the hotel."

"Where's their father?"

"He was out fishing when the killer wave snatched everything in its path. Pieces of his boat washed ashore a few days
later." Jasmira wiped away the tears that streaked her cheeks.

"Please don't cry. Let's sing a happy song."

Jasmira nodded. "Yes, a happy song to help me stop
missing my children."

On the second day, Jasmira woke Oceana. "I'm going to
the beach to search for my children. Will you come help me?
You might see places I missed. Two pairs of eyes are better
than one."

Quickly pulling on her dress, Oceana followed Jasmira
down the path that led to the beach. The sun colored the sky
with vibrant shades of pink and red. Before dawn, hotel workers had picked up litter and raked the sand smooth. By mid-
morning, the beach would be covered with colorful towels and
sun worshippers.

But at this early hour, there were only local people on the
beach. Several walked up and down, pacing back and forth, as
if they were lost.

Jasmira touched Oceana's shoulder. "They're trying to find
their children, too."

Oceana looked at the sad faces of the searchers. They
silently passed around photos of their children. Jasmira
looked through a bundle and shook her head. The crowd
slowly dispersed.

Jasmira's head dropped down to her chest. "I don't know
how much longer I can take this."

"Maybe if you accepted the truth…"

Jasmira cut her off. "No. The truth you see would be unbearable."

"The truth is the truth, no matter who sees it," Oceana said, as if explaining to a child.

"Don't ask that of me. It's too much for me to even consider."

A few stragglers walked toward Jasmira and Oceana. One woman was clutching photos close to her heart. She held them out to Jasmira when she was near enough to show them. "These are my children. Have you seen them?" Her hands trembled as she offered Jasmira the pictures.

Jasmira looked at the photos and shook her head. "No, I'm sorry," she said, looking straight into the distraught woman's eyes.

"If you see them, will you please tell them their Mama is looking for them?"

"Of course," Jasmira answered in a gentle voice. She glanced at the images again.

Soon Jasmira and Oceana were alone on the beach. "I don't think that woman will ever see her children again," Jasmira said.

"What makes you think that?" Oceana asked.

"Just a feeling I have."

"What kind of feeling do you have about your own children?"

"Sometimes I think they're truly gone. But I won't let that thought stay long in my mind. Accepting their death would destroy me."

"But what if it's true?" Oceana kicked up sand with her bare feet, her anklet sparkling in the sunlight.

Jasmira didn't answer but stared out into the dark blue sea. Gentle waves lapped at the shoreline.

A week later as Jasmira and Oceana walked the beach,

Oceana suddenly turned to the woman and clapped her hands. "I have a great idea. Why don't we help people look for their children?"

"What's so great about that?"

"When we go to the shelters to look for their children, maybe we'll find yours."

"I've been to the shelters. Many times."

"Maybe it would help you to help others."

"I don't know what you're talking about." Jasmira turned abruptly and began walking away from Oceana.

But the child ran after her and pulled her arm. "If you're busy helping others, you can't be thinking about your own sorrows."

Jasmira looked down at the child thoughtfully. The sun slashed through the trees and rested on Oceana's upturned face. Her aquamarine eyes shone like jewels. The silver heart at her throat twinkled in the sunlight.

Oceana continued. "We could look carefully at the photos and then search each shelter. If we found one child for a Mama there would be much dancing and singing. And you would know you made it happen."

"I'll think about it. Let's go home now."

For several days no mention was made of Oceana's suggestion. Jasmira continued looking for her children each morning and evening. The table was always set for five. Then, one morning after Jasmira returned from a fruitless search at the beach, she said to Oceana, "I don't have to be at work until this afternoon. Come back with me to the beach and help me look through the photos the desperate ones show around."

"Will we go visit the rescued children in shelters?"

"Of course," Jasmira said as if it were her idea. "Eat first. Then we'll go."

Oceana shook her head. "I'm not hungry. Let's hurry

before the parents leave." She ran out the door, her curly hair flying out behind her. Jasmira had to hurry to keep up with the girl.

At the beach, Jasmira and Oceana looked carefully at some photos. "We will go to a few shelters today and look for your child," the woman said to a distraught man, keeping one of the prints.

He shook his head sadly. "I've been to the shelters and my son isn't in any of them."

Oceana piped up. "I think new children show up each day and they move them to different shelters when no one comes to claim them."

The man's eyes lit up. "I will be here at dawn every day."

Jasmira and Oceana went to four shelters and searched every face, but didn't find the son. "How will I tell the poor man that I failed?" Jasmira asked Oceana.

"You didn't fail. You looked. That was all you could do." She tugged the woman's arm. "We have time for one more shelter."

But the answer was the same. The boy wasn't there.

The next morning, Jasmira walked toward the man displaying his photos to others on the beach. When he saw her draw near, he stood motionless waiting for her to speak. She shook her head. "I'm sorry. I couldn't find him for you."

The man tapped his chest with his fingers. "You touched my heart by helping me look. For that I am grateful." He bowed and walked away.

His words spurred Jasmira on. Every day after that they took a photo from a searcher and visited the shelters. One day, as they were leaving the last shelter Oceana pointed to a child huddled in a corner. "Look, Mama Six. Isn't that the little girl in the picture?"

Jasmira sucked in her breath. She kept looking back and

forth from the photo to the little girl. They found the caretaker and showed her the picture. "Bring the mother as quickly as you can."

"I don't know where she lives, but I'll see her on the beach tomorrow morning. I'll bring her then." Jasmira looked at the caretaker sternly. "Don't let anyone touch that child until we come back tomorrow."

The caretaker nodded. "Of course not. We want to send the children back to their parents."

The following day, Jasmira and Oceana approached the woman who had given her the photo of the girl child. "I think we found your daughter." The woman swayed and Jasmira had to steady her so she wouldn't topple over. They sat the woman down on the sand and fanned her with their hands. When color came back into the mother's face, Jasmira said, "Come with us. We'll take you there."

At the shelter, Jasmira and Oceana watched with tears in their eyes as the woman rushed to her daughter and hugged the little girl to her chest, kissing her over and over, murmuring soft words that only her child could hear. The little girl clung to her mother, digging her tiny hands into her mother's back. Jasmira wiped her eyes at this tender sight.

"Does it make you sad that she has found her child and you haven't found your children?" Oceana asked.

"I must admit that a little sadness has crept into my heart. But my tears are tears of happiness for them."

Oceana smiled and sighed deeply.

Over the next two weeks, Jasmira and Oceana spent every spare moment helping saddened parents look for their children. They found two children from one family and excitedly gave the parents the news. In between thanking Jasmira and hugging her, the mother shrieked hysterically, asking if she were sure the found children were the ones in the photo. "I'm afraid to believe," the distraught woman said as her husband tried to calm her.

Oceana tugged the woman's hand. "I saw them with my own eyes. They're your children," she said. "Hurry. They're waiting for you."

"Thank you, Oceana," Jasmira said to the child on their last night together as they sat down for supper. Only two place settings were laid out on the table.

"For what, Mama Six?"

"For showing me that in helping others look for their children, I was helping myself accept my loss."

"And what does that mean?" Oceana leaned across the table and looked into Jasmira's eyes.

"It means that I have finally accepted that my children are gone. That the killer wave found their hiding place and swept them into the sea." She looked at Oceana with misted eyes. "I am happy for one thing, though."

Oceana leaned closer. "Happy?"

"Yes. The three of them were taken together so they won't be lonely." Oceana squeezed the woman's hand.

Jasmira wiped her eyes with her bare arm. "Let's eat," she said. "We have to get up early tomorrow. I hear they set up a new shelter. We'll go there right after we pick up the photos."

The next morning when Jasmira and Oceana walked on the beach, the woman stopped suddenly and looked around at all the hiding places where she had searched for her children. Then shading her eyes, she turned and looked out to the sea.

"Mama Six?" Oceana said in a questioning voice.

Jasmira put a hand on Oceana's small shoulder and with the other, blew a kiss toward the ocean. "You will always be in my heart," she whispered. Then turning to Oceana she smiled and said, "Let's go help the other parents find their children."

And so Oceana and Jasmira walked side by side to the far

end of the beach where a group of people clutched precious photos close to their hearts.

Letting Go

Mama Seven

Kirti sat on the dirt floor of her tin and thatched-roof dwelling made from discarded materials. Her dark pinched face was deep in concentration as she counted coins. The cupboards used to be overflowing with bags of rice and other foodstuff, but the killer wave had come like a thief and snatched everything from her. Her three children. Her husband. Her home and all its contents.

She had cried out against the fates, beat her head against the wall. No matter what she did, the sea did not return her family. They were lost to her forever. They could never be replaced. But her possessions could if she were thrifty and careful with her money. Kirti had already begun stockpiling. Early mornings were spent scavenging the beach. She hoped Oceana didn't eat much.

Kirti heaved her heavy body to her feet to wait for the girl. Standing in the doorway, her beady eyes spotted Oceana walking up the dirt path, kicking up dust with her bare feet, swinging her arms up and down.

She was coming empty-handed.

Oceana had no sooner walked through the doorway when Kirti asked, "Where are the dresses Kamalika made you?"

"I gave three to Mama Two for the little ones she's keeping. And I'm wearing one." She spun around to show off her favorite, the now-faded poppy-red dress.

"That's four."

"Mama Six is washing my other dress and will bring it later."

"You go right back and get those three dresses from Hema. They were made for you, not for waifs."

"I don't need them," Oceana protested.

"No matter. They're yours."

"Mama Seven, I can only wear one dress at a time."

The woman shook her head. "You need to be prudent."

Oceana giggled. "I don't know what that means but it sounds awful." She pushed back the dark ringlets that had fallen across her face. "Anyhow, I want the little ones to feel special by having pretty clothes to wear."

Kirti's face hardened as she shook her head in disbelief.

After a scanty lunch, Kirti grunted as she plopped down and began counting her coins once again. Oceana sat down next to her on the floor. "What are you doing" she asked.

"Counting my money."

"Why?"

"So I know how much I have saved." Kirti separated the coins by denominations.

"Why are you saving your money?" Oceana reached out to

touch a shiny coin. Kirti swatted her hand.

"So I'll have it when I need it. You never know what's around the corner." She moved the coins away from Oceana and said, "And don't touch my money."

"The lady down the path called you a miser. What does that mean?"

"What's mine is mine," Kirti announced firmly.

Oceana looked around the small dwelling. Overflowing boxes took up much of the space. Some broken boxes held foodstuff, some old newspapers, some trinkets. Dust covered the whole lot. "Why are you saving these things?"

Kirti sat with her pudgy hands on her rounded hips and surveyed her possessions. "You just never know what you're going to need. If I give something away, I'm sure to need it the next day."

"But Mama Seven, you can't possibly use all this." Oceana swung her hands out wide.

"And you can't be sure of that. I feel more comfortable surrounded by bits and pieces that might be of use some day."

"That's holding onto fear." Oceana picked up a dusty bag of rice. "Someone who is hungry could eat this."

"And what if I use up all my food and I need that bag of rice you're dangling?"

Oceana blew off the dust and sneezed.

Kirti yanked the rice from Oceana's hands. "These things are mine and I intend to keep them." She stared into the girl's sea-green eyes. "We'll get along much better this month if you don't interfere in my business." She threw the rice back into the box.

A few days later, Kirti said to Oceana, "After breakfast I want you to help me search the beach for things tourists leave behind."

"Things?"

"Yes, things. Didn't you understand me?" Kirti squinted at Oceana through narrowed, puffy eyes.

"I understood the words but I don't understand why you want things that belong to someone else."

"Just do as you're told and stop questioning me."

"I don't think…"

Holding up her hands, Kirti said, "Don't say another word. After breakfast we *will* go to the beach."

When they sat down to eat, Oceana said, "Mama Seven, can I have some of those crackers?" She pointed to a box on a small wooden crate.

"No, I might want them later. Eat this bread." She shoved a stale loaf of bread across the table. Oceana dipped the bread in her tea until it was soggy.

"Hurry, I want to start out before it gets too hot. And I have to work at the hotel this afternoon." She brushed her hands together greedily. "Maybe a rich tourist will give me something nice today to add to my stack." She pointed to a box in the corner filled with clothes and purses and shoes. A few pieces of costume jewelry hung over the sides.

"Do you wear any of that?" Oceana asked, going over to the box.

"Don't be silly. Most of the rich tourists are skinny." Kirti patted her wide hips and then looked down at her fat, swollen feet.

"Mama One could make dresses and shirts for orphans who need clothes."

Kirti shook her head. "You keep your hands away from my things. Don't be giving anything away without my permission. Some day I might lose weight and then I'll need those clothes."

Tilting her head, Oceana asked, "Do you keep everything you get?"

Kirti wore a puzzled expression on her face. "Why

wouldn't I? Now, if you're finished eating, let's search the beach."

Oceana followed Kirti down the dusty path that curved before it reached the sea. "What's that over there?" the woman asked, panting from exertion as she pointed to the side of the trail.

Oceana skipped over to the area. She knelt down and then exclaimed, "Oh, Mama Seven, look. A baby bird. Something must be wrong with his wing. He's trying to fly but can't. Can we take him home until he gets bigger and stronger? Please?"

Kirti lumbered over to Oceana and gazed eagerly at the young bird the girl held in her small hands. What a great addition to her collection of novelties. She had a small cage around somewhere and the bird would make a fine pet. Not liking dogs and being allergic to cats made the bird a nice alternative.

"Forget the search. Bring him along. I have just the place for him by my bed."

"But you'll let him go when he gets better, won't you?" Oceana asked, petting the bird's tiny head.

"Of course not. We found him. He's ours."

"It's a wild bird, Mama Seven. It needs to be free." Oceana's eyes matched the color of the rolling ocean's waves.

"Don't be silly. We'll tame him. I'll get him to perch on my shoulder."

Oceana walked purposefully over to Kirti. "That's mean. The bird needs to be set free when he can fly."

"If we feed him and give him water, he won't want to fly away. You'll see. Now let's hurry home so I can find that cage before I leave for the hotel."

Oceana murmured softly to the bird and Kirti caught snatches of her words, *Trust me, I'll help you. You were meant to be free.* The woman chose not to comment on Oceana's ramblings. They would keep the bird no matter what that child told it.

At the dwelling Kirti dug through one of the boxes, scattering junk all over the floor. "Here it is," she shouted. She held up a small, dented cage.

Oceana looked on in horror as if she couldn't bear to think of the poor little bird locked up in an old rusted cage. "I'll take care of you," she said softly as the bird burrowed into the folded dress that Jasmira must have left on Oceana's sleeping mat.

"I have to go to work now. Here's some water and bread to feed the bird. Put him in the cage." She hurried out the doorway.

Kirti shook her head as she turned and watched Oceana bring the food over to the mat. The bird raised its head and opened its mouth to take the softened bread from the girl's hand. Kirti quickly walked up the path to the hotel. She didn't have time to chastise the girl, but she would when she returned from work.

It was her house. Her rules. And her bird.

Kirti was sure she had a disease that made her get fatter over the months. She didn't eat much although she did like the sweets left by the tourists. It seemed to her that it was around the time she began collecting things that she started gaining weight. And just as she was unable to let go of her possessions, she was unable to shed the extra pounds from her body.

Oceana wasn't the first one to urge her to get rid of some of her things. And while she occasionally considered it, in the end she couldn't bear to part with one solitary item. Not the smallest piece of paper, not the oldest scrap of food.

She was happiest when she was collecting. It wasn't so much the items as the feelings they stirred within her. Safety. Control. Security. And even though Oceana annoyed her with her questions, Kirti wondered how she'd be able to let her go at the end of the month. Well, she wouldn't worry about that now. She had lots of time to think about it and work something out.

When Kirti walked into the dwelling, the first thing she saw was the bird lying on a scrunched up dress on Oceana's lap. The girl was singing to the bird that looked up at her as if it knew the song was for him. Oceana's aquamarine eyes glowed with happiness as she touched the bird's head gently. The cage was still on the floor where Kirti had left it.

"The bird's mine," Kirti said.

"The bird doesn't belong to anyone. He's here for us to take care of until he can fly."

"The way you're fawning over it, I don't think you'll be in such a hurry to let it go."

Oceana smiled. "I will when the time is right. I don't need to own anything."

"You own two dresses, don't you? And the anklet. And what about that chain around your neck with the little dangling heart? You never take it off." Kirti walked inside and stood over Oceana.

"Yes, but I was happy before I had those things."

Kirti wore that puzzled expression again. "How can you be happy without owning anything?" She swung her flabby arms wide. "After the killer wave took my three children and my husband and washed away all my possessions, I was quick to gather up everything I could find. It helped fill the empty space in my heart. That is what makes me happy."

Oceana looked at her sadly. "No, it just clutters your heart. Other people could have used some of what you found. You have more than you need." She touched the bird's head. "Sometimes when you hold on tightly you can't tell the difference between the good and the bad. And then you begin collecting what's bad."

"Well, I have been feeling ill lately. So some of the food must have gone bad." Kirti looked down at herself. "And there's all this extra weight I carry around."

"Maybe if you start letting go of some of the things you don't need or use, you'll feel better."

Kirti shook her head and glanced at the bird. "Put him in the cage."

"He needs to stay close to me so I can feed him as often as his mama would."

"You're not his mama."

"We are all many things."

Biting back the retort on her lips, Kirti's eyes narrowed as she looked at Oceana. Then she sucked in her breath at the sight before her. Light from outside shone on the girl's head, giving off a halo effect. The ethereal vision made Kirti clamp her mouth shut.

When Oceana moved from the light and Kirti gained her composure, she said, "If we are many things, what are you?"

"I'm the bird's friend."

"I think you're as obsessed with that bird as I am with my possessions."

Oceana shook her head. "I know I can't hold onto something that wants to be free. I can only take care of it while it's with me. Then I have to let it go."

"We'll see." Kirti made a pot of soup and put the box of crackers on the table. "Help yourself," she said to Oceana.

After eating, Kirti said, "Let's go to the market. You're not too young to learn how to shop wisely."

Women milled around the stalls at the marketplace. Next to the food, salvaged materials scattered the ground. There was no laughter or music ever since the killer wave had shredded souls. Women with bowed heads weighed the food silently.

Kirti looked around before heading toward some children selling rice. She drove a hard bargain, giving them much less than what they had originally asked for. She smirked. "That's how it's done."

Oceana looked back at the sad faces of the young boys. She tugged Kirti's arm. "Can I have a coin?"

"So you want to try your hand at the game?"

Oceana smiled and held out her hand.

Kirti placed a shiny coin in the girl's small palm. "Let's see how many items you can get."

Oceana spotted a man selling nuts. She skipped over to him and bought a bag of mixed nuts. Quickly she retraced her steps until she found the boys who had sold Kirti the rice. "These are for you," she said, handing them the bag.

The boys looked up in surprise. They took the nuts and quickly hid them under a sack of rice. "She's going to be mad at you," they said, pointing to Kirti. "Will she beat you?"

"Maybe."

"Aren't you afraid?" the older boy asked.

Oceana shook her head and her dark ringlets danced around her face. "You can't be afraid when your heart is right." She left the boys and went to find Kirti.

"So what did you buy?" Kirti asked, eyeing Oceana's empty hands.

"I bought nuts." The soft murmur of the market surrounded them.

"Where are they? Did you eat them all?" Kirti's eyes locked with Oceana's. "I will be very upset if you did."

"I gave them to the boys you cheated."

Kirti's eyes bulged and her hand whipped out and struck Oceana. "You took my money and gave it away?"

"No, you gave it to me so it was my money. And I bought nuts for the boys." Oceana rubbed her cheek.

Kirti grabbed the girl's arm, pinching it, and dragged her out of the marketplace. "You'll go without supper tonight and no breakfast tomorrow. And when your stomach is growling with hunger you can think about how foolish you were to give away food."

The next morning, Kirti said to Oceana, "Are you sorry you gave those boys the nuts when you could have been eating them right now?"

Oceana shook her head. "They were hungry, Mama Seven. I had to do it."

"I don't understand you. We don't have much food."

"There's always enough to share."

"Not from this house."

Oceana walked over to Kirti and touched her arm. "When you give from your heart, it always comes back to you."

"Nonsense."

Days went by and Oceana never put the bird in the cage. Kirti refrained from commenting on this oversight. Instead, she found herself asking if she could hold the bird once in a while. The girl always offered the bird graciously. It hadn't yet flown but it seemed bigger and stronger.

Now that her back was beginning to ache, Kirti thought about letting go some of the tourist clothes to see if that would make a difference as Oceana had suggested. Kirti even carried some of the dresses to the market but found she was unable to part with them. She was afraid she might need them one day. It was then that she began to realize her possessions had some kind of hold on her. Maybe if the girl accompanied her she'd be able to follow through and get rid of some things. She could always start with a small trinket and see how that went.

On the way to the market, Oceana said, "It's not just giving something away. You must let go of your thoughts about things." Oceana kicked up dust with her bare feet. The wind rustled her curly hair and she pushed it out of her eyes. "You don't have to keep it all. It's letting go that makes you free."

"But supposing I give something away and then I find I need it?" She scratched her leg. These conversations always made her anxious.

"We *need* very little. Most of it we *want*."

One evening after they finished supper, Kirti said to Oceana, "I've given away a whole box of things. But I still get a rash. And I still feel anxious. Why is that?"

"Because you only give away what you don't want. You didn't let go of your attachment." She pointed to the boxes still piled high.

"You haven't let go of your attachment to that bird either," Kirti said indignantly.

Oceana smiled. "I will when he's ready to fly."

"And he's going to tell you?" Kirti snickered.

Giggling behind her hand, Oceana said, "Not in words. But he'll tell me."

"Enough about the bird. How do I let go of my attachments?" She looked around the room at her beloved possessions that felt like a safety net.

"Pick something you like that would make someone else happy. Then give it away. Ask for nothing, not even a thank you."

"But supposing they don't appreciate it like I do?" Kirti began scratching her leg.

"Letting go can be scary, but once you let something go, it's not yours anymore. The person can throw it away. Or hold it close to their heart. But what they do with it has nothing to do with you."

"This is too difficult. I couldn't bear it if they didn't like something I gave them." She shook her head. "No, I can't do it."

Oceana got up and put her cheek next to Kirti's. "Yes, you can. It's not that hard. And each time you do it, it will get easier."

Kirti deliberated for several days. Then, piece by piece she gave the contents in the box that the tourists had given her to the beggars in the marketplace. Several times she had to talk herself into letting an item go, especially if it were silky or beaded. But in the end, the box was empty.

"How do you feel?" Oceana asked when she saw the box lying on its side in front of the dwelling.

"My shoulders don't droop anymore. And I feel lighter." Kirti looked down at her rounded body and laughed. "I know I didn't lose any weight, but I don't feel the heaviness I felt when I was hanging on to everything. My rash has cleared up, too."

"There are a lot more boxes in there," Oceana said, pointing to the dwelling.

"Well, aren't you the pushy one. I thought you'd be thrilled with what I've done." Kirti stomped into the house. Oceana followed her inside.

"You did great. But there are a lot more attachments you have to let loose."

"Why is it so important for me to let everything go?"

"When you free yourself of things, you free yourself."

"So the things I had hoarded were weighing me down?"

"I think that's why you feel lighter and your shoulders don't droop."

"Help me get rid of this stuff. I'm going to offer it to the unfortunate ones. Except for what I really need." She smiled at Oceana. "I do believe I could walk on air."

Oceana giggled. "You're funny, Mama Seven."

Weeks later when all the things were given away, Kirti said to Oceana. "There's one more."

Letting Go

"One more?"

Kirti nodded. "The bird."

Oceana's eyes misted. "Yes, the bird. He can fly now."

"Do you want to do it?" Kirti asked.

Oceana shook her head, her eyes glistening with tears. "Let's both take him. We'll walk down the path where we found him."

Oceana held the small bird in her hands and talked to him as they walked. "You're going to be free to find your mama. She will welcome you and love you." Tears fell from her eyes onto the bird's face. He opened his mouth to drink in the moisture.

When they came to the place where Oceana had found him, she kissed his little head and handed him to Kirti. "It's only right that you set him free."

Kirti gently took the bird. She looked from him to Oceana several times. Oceana nodded. Kirti lifted her hands. "Fly, little bird. I'm letting you go."

The bird fluttered his wings and flew away. Kirti and Oceana watched until they could no longer see him. Then Oceana laced her fingers with Kirti's and the two walked hand in hand back to the dwelling.

Seven Healing Women

The seven women huddled together, their dark heads touching, and decided on a celebration. Seven months had passed since Oceana had come into their lives and they wanted to do something special for the child before starting her month-long rotations again. While they still mourned their children, each had been transformed in myriad ways. They attributed this transformation to Oceana.

They would hold the party on the beach where Oceana first appeared to them. There would be food and music and games. The women chose a Wednesday, the quietest day at the hotel, and were granted the afternoon off.

They spent many days in preparation. Festive clothes had to be made, food prepared, games chosen. Oceana, who was staying with Kirti until after the celebration, insisted on wearing her faded poppy-red dress with a border of small blue and white flowers embroidered around the hem.

When the day of the party arrived, they gathered at Kamalika's dwelling. Carrying trays of food and jugs of water, they walked the path to the beach, Oceana skipping ahead, the dog trotting by her side. Oceana sang and her young voice carried back to the women. One by one they joined in.

The women knew this day was quite different from that day seven months prior when they had been staring hopelessly at the sea. Today their sadness was banished. The women sang, and laughed, and smiled. They were happy.

The afternoon sped by. Once the food was eaten and the games played, the women began cleaning up. Oceana called out, "I'm going into the sea." She hugged each Mama and then kissed their suntanned cheeks. Frolicking and playing with the dog, she ran into the ocean and jumped up and down splashing herself. The laughing women waved to her and she waved back.

Suddenly, the surf washed over Oceana and she slipped out of sight. The anxious women waited for her to surface. Then, their joy turned into fear. They picked up their skirts and ran to the water's edge.

"Oceana," they cried out. "Where are you?" Ushma and Jasmira, who could swim, tore off their skirts and dove into the water. The others shielded their eyes from the glare of the sun, hoping to see Oceana resurface. The dog lay down on the sand with his paws crossed, looking out toward the sea.

Kirti stood back a little from the others, not because she was too heavy to swim in the ocean, but because a small bird had perched on a bush nearby claiming her attention. Her heart skipped a beat. She was sure it was the bird she and Oceana had rescued. He flew to Kirti's shoulder and twittered

in her ear.

Kirti wrung her shaking hands. "What are you trying to tell me?"

The bird flew around her, going from one bush to another, circling her, repeating his flight pattern. His movements mesmerized Kirti. Suddenly the bird took flight and soared over the sea until she could no longer see him.

Kirti swayed as she remembered her conversation with Oceana. *'You haven't let go of your attachment,' Oceana had said. 'You haven't let go of your attachment to that bird either,' Kirti had countered. 'I will when he's ready to fly.' Kirti remembered snickering. 'And he's going to tell you?' she'd asked. 'Not in words. But he'll tell me.'*

The women who had stayed on shore helped Ushma and Jasmira struggling out of the sea. "We can't find her," Jasmira gasped, choking on the salt water she'd swallowed. The six women dropped to the sand. Then their eyes were drawn to Kirti, who stood several feet away from them, motionless, as if in a trance.

Suddenly Kirti raised her arms and spoke. "Oceana taught me that you cannot hold on to someone who wants to be free. You can only love them for the short time they are with you. Then you must let them go." One by one Kirti looked into the eyes of each woman. "Oceana came to us from the sea and has chosen to return to its depths. We have to let her go."

The dog began barking and the seven women whirled around. A ray of sunlight had slashed through the clouds and lit up the water where Oceana had last been seen. Kamalika turned to the others. "It reminds me of the light that sometimes glowed around Oceana." The others nodded in agreement. They looked again to the sea, now calm and peaceful. The sun had slipped once again behind the clouds.

Madhur bit down on her lip and blinked several times to

clear the tears that blurred her vision. With a voice barely audible she said, "Our beloved Oceana belongs to the sea, not to us."

The other women murmured amongst themselves.

Gaining her composure once more, Kirti called out, "Remember, this is a celebration of love for Oceana. We must not grieve for her. She would not want that."

And so the women huddled together for several minutes. Then led by Madhur, they nodded in agreement. Separating, the seven women gathered all the colorful flowers and blossoms nearby and threw them into the deep. They watched the waves snatch their offerings until the ocean swallowed up the flora. Even the little dog picked up a stick and dropped it in the water.

When the women turned from the sea and walked on the sun-warmed sand, Hema kicked something shiny. Bending down slowly, she picked up the silver chain with the puffed heart that Oceana had never taken off. Hema blinked back tears. She held up the necklace for the others to see, and then slipped it into her pocket until later.

Kamalika suddenly cried out, "Oceana taught me how to live again with love in my heart." She placed her hand on the little dog's head.

"She taught me how to leave darkness behind to find joy," said Hema, twirling around as Oceana had often done.

Ushma raised her hands up to the sky. "I believe the spirit of our children sent Oceana to help us heal," she said.

The other women's faces lit up. "Yes," they echoed.

"Because of Oceana, I was able to find it in my heart to forgive my sister," added Gulika.

Madhur looked down sheepishly. "My eyes were opened to be thankful for everything I have, especially my friends."

"In helping others, I was finally able to accept the death of my children," said Jasmira.

The six women turned to Kirti. "Today, Oceana taught us all about letting go." Then she waved her hands to keep their attention. "When Oceana hugged me before she went into the sea, she whispered, *"'I was blessed to have seven wonderful Mamas.'"*

With tears in their eyes, the women beamed and clapped their hands.

Kirti raised her arms again to silence the women. "But there was something else she wanted us to know."

The women looked at Kirti expectantly.

"Oceana wanted us to share what we learned with the villagers."

The women nodded eagerly.

Then, in a circle, they put their arms around each other and with one last look at the sea, turned and walked hand in hand to the village, the little dog trotting beside them.